BEASTINGS

Praise for Benjamin Myers' writing

"His poetic vernacular brims with that quality most sadly lost – humanity." *The Guardian*

"Pig Iron is an important book because it tells a story that has shaped all contemporary Western humans, but is routinely, inexplicably overlooked - the great move from agricultural life to industrial life." *Deborah Orr*

"A novelist who is unafraid to explore the wider terrain of fiction. In searching further than most contemporary novelists he has produced a novel of staggering voice, feeling and wit." *Lee Rourke*

"Pig Iron deserves to find itself on many a reading list, if not the National Curriculum." *3:AM Magazine*

"An excellent book...never once is there a dropped beat." *The Times*

"A moving, tender novel." *Marie Claire*

"Myers is a sensitive, thoughtful writer. His greatest skill is the atmospheric evocation of landscape and place." *Owen Hatherley*

"Extraordinary." *Daily Mirror*

"Brutality and beauty co-exist easily on the page and remind us that there are still original and urgent voices out there creating new and exciting fiction." *Loud & Quiet*

"Benjamin Myers's influences are clear — David Peace's northern brutalism is evident and there are suggestions of Salinger and Golding but Pig Iron's savage vision is his alone." *Morning Star*

"Myers has an elegant turn of phrase and there are moments of haunting poetry." *Metro*

"Slashes and burns its way through the bloated beigeness of the contemporary British novel." *Bookmunch*

"The ending came in a sudden flash of gold and beauty. To say more would be to give it away; suffice to say, you'll like it when you get there and it's a journey worth making." *Sam Jordison*

"It's a brilliant book and I loved it." *The Sun*

"Brilliant." *Dazed & Confused*

BEASTINGS

By

Benjamin Myers

Bluemoose

First published in 2014 by
Bluemoose Books Ltd
25 Sackville Street
Hebden Bridge
West Yorkshire
HX7 7DJ

www.bluemoosebooks.com

British Library Cataloguing-in-Publication data
A catalogue record for this book is available from the British Library

Paperback ISBN 978 0 9927919 3 3

Hardback ISBN 978 0 9927919 4 0

Printed and bound in the UK by Short Run Press

For my parents
who showed
me the mountains.

"He gives the barren woman a home, making her the joyous mother of children. Praise the Lord."

~ Psalms 113:9

WHEN THE MOON was a pearl at the bottom of the tarn they walked over drifts of shifting shale and wild waxy grass polished to a sheen by the wind and when the great banks of cloud rolled in and they could see neither their hands in front of their faces nor their feet on the ground they sat where they were and waited it out.

Once when they were walking the Priest stopped and raised a hand as if to swear an oath and said listen and the Poacher said what do you hear and the Priest said just listen and they stood in silence then the Priest said I can hear a baby crying and from the far distance along the broad fell and across the tight valley they could hear the shrill unfettered screams of a creature in distress.

That's them said the Priest that's the child and the Poacher said that's not them and the Priest said how do you know and the Poacher said because that's not a baby that's two foxes rutting mark my words – that's two foxes at it – mating like – I'd know that sound anywhere. I've heard it a thousand times before and I expect I'll hear it a thousand times more. What happens is the vixen clamps on and the dog swells inside her and it's him what makes the screaming not her. The Priest said are you sure because that sounds like a baby to me and the Poacher said it may sound like a bairn but that's foxes trust me Father though many is the night wanderer that's made the same mistake as you.

· They listened some more to the howls of pain that cut through the night like the sound of something human being torn apart. A sound to freeze hot blood and still a beating heart.

Then they pressed on.

1.

RAIN FELL LIKE steel rivets.

It came down hard pile-driving into the ground. It was the first full fall in the weeks since she had left St Mary's.

She had departed while the embers were still glowing. Upped and went before Hinckley started hacking in his pit. She'd bundled the bairn and gone out the back way. Taken one of the tracks out of town. Away from the streets and into the trees.

It was best for the both of them. To get out of that house. The only way.

She had known it the first moment she saw him lift the baby. The way he had held it all wrong and shaken it when it cried. Shouting all the time in its face so that his voice went hoarse. It was a tiny thing; a fragile thing. It would only be a matter of time before those hands – hands used to smashing rock and hewing stone – would go too far. She saw a life that was already set in place just as hers was set from day one.

The child was a rare and delicate egg that had fallen from a crooked nest.

There were places they could go to beyond the horizon where she had heard that things were different; stories of the seaside and great mountains made from sand and boats just sitting there waiting to be sailed away.

Some of the Sisters – the ones with the strangest accents – had talked of an island out there. They said it was free of serpents. Maybe there were other islands too. Maybe there were other islands that were empty where she and the bairn could live safely in silence.

Because on an island in the ocean no-one can sneak up on you.

It would be some time before they missed the bairn or did anything about it. Of this she was certain. They weren't even fussed; anyone could see that. Might be that they'd come after her; might be they'd see it as a blessing. Certainly he didn't give a fig for the child. They had a head start at least.

And now it was raining and the girl was under the cover of branches but she was wet and already shivering and soon the trees would end and the fells would begin and after that she would just keep moving. One foot and then the other.

After many hours the rain slowed and the girl spied the tops of a cluster of buildings in the distance. She went towards them.

Through the falling cords of drizzle she saw that it was a farm dwelling hunched in a hollow in the ground. It held one house and a number of outbuildings.

The girl approached from behind and had to climb over a stone wall and push through furze that stabbed at her and then she was in the farm yard. She looked from left to right. She waited. A man stepped out from the barn. A dog followed behind him. The dog's ears were standing to attention and it circled the yard low stalking the ground. It had smelled the girl first then heard her. Sight was the third sense.

The man looked up and saw her and the collie growled. He gave a curt but shrill whistle and it crouched onto its stomach.

The man slowly walked towards the girl. He stopped and squinted at her through the rain. The dog suppressed a growl.

What you after said the man.

The girl looked over her shoulder back the way she had come to check her escape route in case he came at her.

She pulled the bundle tight to her chest.

You're a long way from anywhere here.

His voice was loud. It cut through the space between them. He spoke at the volume of someone who lived outdoors someone more used to talking to dogs and cows and sheep.

You must be after summat he said.

The rain was teeming now. It was running in rivulets from the rim of the man's hat. She had never seen one like it before.

The dog's fur was matted into points and its ears flattened down. It hadn't taken its eyes off her.

Trying to get to the lake he said. A statement.

She nodded. Uncertain.

It's slewing it. Bad day for you and the bairn to be out.

The girl looked at the bundle then back over her shoulder and then she turned her head to the man. He stared but she refused to meet his eyes; she could only look vaguely towards his form.

The man stepped closer to her. He was wearing an old pair of Hessian boots that went up to just below the knee. The girl chewed at her lower lip.

He saw the unsuitable boots on her feet that were caked in mud to her ankles. And still she wouldn't meet his eyes.

The bairn'll be after feeding he said.

The girl said nothing so he turned to the house and without looking back said there's milk indoors.

He walked across the yard but the dog stayed for a moment then he whistled and it turned and followed him. So did the girl.

There was a run-off down one side of the yard and it was thick with slurry. The flow carried the detritus of the yard: straw and effluent and dampened clumps of grist.

The farmer walked around to the side of the house and opened the door.

The girl paused a pace behind.

Come on then if you're coming.

He turned and she followed through the doorway and into the scullery. It was a dark room and no warmer than outside but it was dry.

Her boots rattled on the slate.

There was a stone sink and straw underfoot to mop up the mud that they had trailed in from the yard. More straw in the corner to make a nest for the dog. Cured meat parts turned on chains that hung from ceiling hooks. Ham sides and bacon flanks. She held the baby tighter to her chest.

She followed the man through to the kitchen and as she did he stopped and turned to her and she flinched but he was only closing the door to keep the dog out of the main trunk of the house. It scratched at the closed door but the man said get by in a low voice and it quietened down.

The kitchen led onto a small living room. There was no door between the rooms only a low stone arch.

The man bent to stoke the hot coals in the range then pushed a handful of kindling in and pulled a metal stopper to fan the embers. The flames took to the branches. Then he picked up the scuttle and rattled more coal into the stove. The fire jumped into life and the sound of the cracking coal and the smell of the coke dust and the shadows on the dark walls put her back there. Back to the time before Hinckley and before the Sisters even; back to the house of her parents up top. A world of shadows and sounds and smells and feelings rather than clear images. Tension and fear and pain.

Her parents were a storm rolling over the tops; their pairing was a flash of violence and the crack of the sky in the cramped room where the fire burned. The sound of slapping and stamping. A family activity was gathering to watch a sheep have its throat slit out front. The gleeful chatter of hungry voices as the black blood dripped into a bucket and the face of the animal as its eyes searched the crowd for an explanation were as memorable now as if it were yesterday yet the face of her father had been reduced to nothing but a smudge. A rough-edged shape.

Her mother was a flour-dusted toothless thing who one day turned her back and kept it turned till the church cart and its passengers had crossed the bog on the cart track and disappeared down out of sight. Her tapped daughter gone with it.

By that next spring the rest of the dormitory beds were full with the wild children of the fells now locked in tied down strapped and scratched and starved into shape. Time distorted and time crumbled. Her existence at St Mary's came to be defined by a few stock symbols – soap and scars and slopping out; buckets and bruises and The Book. Life was one hard day followed by the next and for the girl the days stacked up to become first months then years and soon everything that had gone before diminished to a few stock memories. The past was blurred and no-one ever came to bring her back to a hill-top house haunted by past doings like this one here.

So now she would do for the Hinckley bairn what someone should have done for her. Find a way out.

There's tea mashed said the man.

He pulled an armchair over to the range then gestured to it.

The girl sat.

The farmer stood over her. Studied her face for clues.

The bairn'll be wanting summat other than tea though he said.

She looked up at him.

There's milk he said. That's one thing we've plenty of. Milk and bloody mud.

He went into the scullery and came back with a jug and poured some milk into a small pan and placed it on the range then he poured tea.

That's the beastings he said. The mother's first milk for the newborn. The best bit. Tit-fresh.

The girl felt her face flush. The range was kicking out some good heat and the baby stirred a little. Its eyes flickered and its fingers curled around the girl's thumb.

Dry them boots the man said. Else you'll get the toe rot.

The girl shook her head.

No?

The girl shook her head.

Please yourself.

He put his tea down on the side.

I've got things to be doing fore it gets dark he said.

The girl looked up at him and brushed a strand of dark hair from her face. The baby gripped her finger more tightly.

You can stop in till the bairn's fed and you've had a warm but that's it.

The girl's face said nothing.

His voice hardened.

And don't be thinking of taking owt because Ruby'll be in on you in a flash.

The farmer looked at her with scorn then turned and muttered.

Bloody hill wanderers he said.

He left through the scullery. The fire crackled and the girl leaned into the wall of warmth and felt her face flush again.

NIGHT HAD FRAMED St Mary's on the crest in the early hours of the morning that they turned her out for good: an obsidian black pointed block set against the darkest blue.

At the sink the girl had seen the lights coming on across the town one by one. She could just make out the jagged line of the mountains looming like the great scaly back of a dormant beast that would one day awake and rise and swipe the town with a single brush of a limb.

Then after that the buildings the people the Sisters and Father. Especially Father. Everything would be gone.

When that day came St Mary's and everything inside its walls would be nothing but a bad memory. The stones cleaved from the hills above that made the buildings would tumble into the river and the river would dam and flood and the silly statues of the town would fall and the beasts from the farms would run free again. Oak beams would crack and splinter like match sticks. The old bridge would crumble and the banks would wash away. As was prophesied there would be landslides and worse: *by fire and sword he will punish all the people of the world whom he finds guilty – and many will be put to death.*

She pictured it. She prayed for it. She willed it: flames from kilns and ovens would rage and rooftops would fall inwards and not even the rising waters would quell the fires that would burn long into the night and through the next day and those that managed to survive would flee screaming and the town would slowly disappear and all that would be left would be blackened puddles piles of stones and the smell of sulphur. Bodies everywhere and the mountains watching on.

And the Lord says the worms that eat them will never die and the fire that burns them will never be put out. The sight of them will be disgusting to all people.

She had thought about that moment at least once a day for however long she had been kept at St. Mary's. So many years of cold water washes and carbolic soap. Of taunts about her wicked flesh and threats and slaps and midnight violations. Pinned down and pressed back. Gagged.

And now in each window life was happening. Behind curtains people were washing and eating and yawning.

The girl re-focused her eyes and saw herself reflected in the glass. She saw something blank-faced and puffy around the edges. Eyelids still heavy with sleep and a gormless mouth with wet lips. Eyebrows that nearly met in the middle.

She bent and cupped some water then rubbed it into her face. She looked at her reflection and then through that to the town again and the pallid sky above slowly getting lighter and below it the great mountainous beast buried deep in sleep just waiting to make its move. She silently urged it on.

SISTER HAD TOLD her to get some things and when she had got her things Sister said come come in all labour there is profit and whoever sows bountifully will also reap bountifully and then they went outside.

They walked down the hill into fading darkness. She was offered no explanation. No choice. The forces once again guiding her life and determining her existence.

As she left St Mary's behind the girl had felt no relief. No sense of anything ending. The ties to Father were strong whatever he had done because his was a unique protection. Father was doing God's work and He had decided that only Father could lay his hands and everything else upon her.

Out here though.

Out here the threat of the wider world – the threat of what might be – was great. And after so many years living within its shadows each step away from St Mary's only tightened her throat and knotted her stomach.

Sister had moved quickly then. Harried the girl. There was urgency in her movements. Anger.

Don't slouch she said.

Keep up she said.

Sister walked as if the outside world was a dangerous and volatile place and everyone was Satan's hand-maid and the sooner she got back to the orphanage the safer. All the Sisters did. The town was something to be endured – a series of tests of faith – nothing more. Its inhabitants were decadent and vain. No good could ever come of them.

It had been a long time since the girl had been down the hill. Mary's was all she knew and yet here they were – their feet on flat stones as squat square buildings rose up around them. Buildings bigger than she had ever known.

They passed the butcher's window strewn with meat mobiles; hanging forms of plucked parts. Beheaded chickens pig ribs pork chops and offal trays. Dirt-smudged eggs placed around the border. They passed the bakers with its fresh baked loaves buns and cakes. Then the White Lion not yet open for sinners and Sodomites; the pump house by the beck. Over the hump-back bridge to the Co-operative. Then the chemists. The new theatre.

The girl wanted to stop and smell the air and look at things but Sister grabbed her by the elbow and pinched hard and the girl had stumbled and her suitcase had caught between her legs and she nearly fell. Sister only pinched harder.

They left main street and turned into one of the side avenues that pointed down to the lake. The girl still struggling to keep up. Her suitcase clattering against her shins.

Don't pant said Sister. You're not a beast of the field.

Wipe your lip she said.

Close that mouth.

And then they were at the door of a house and Sister was briskly flapping the letterbox and then stepping back and straightening her corners and looking at the girl sideways and saying stand up straight and get rid of that gormless look else I belt it off.

And so began her outside life.

THE CHILD WAS fed and dozing and so was the girl when the farmer returned to stoke the fire and make more tea.

He removed his hat and jacket and hung them on a rusted six inch nail driven into the door back.

He poured them a cup of tea each.

Go through there.

He nodded to the living room.

Sit on one of them other chairs. Else the bairn'll burn up.

The girl didn't move. It was as if his words hadn't registered.

Move he said. I need to be at the range.

She slowly stood and carried the baby into the front room and then sat.

He stoked the fire one more time and when it was glowing he went into the pantry and came out with a jug a bowl of cold boiled potatoes and an onion. The dog followed him.

He chopped the onion and put it into a pot with a knob of butter then set the pot on the range.

When the onion had fried he put the boiled potatoes in and left them for a few minutes then added some of the colostrum from the jug. The girl watched him.

He lifted the pot off the heat and mashed the contents together with the back of a ladle then spooned out two large portions on plates.

He went back to the pantry and came out with a piece of ham. He cut off two thick slices and tossed them into the pot and moved them round in the butter with a fork. While they warmed he cut a round of bread.

The girl and the dog both watched him. The dog stood by his side until he said get by and then it went through to the other room and lay down and watched the girl watch the baby.

The farmer lifted the ham out of the pot with a fork and dropped a slice onto each plate and then he put the plates on the table. He put the slices of bread beside them.

Scran he said and when the girl didn't move he sat down and started to eat.

Scran he said again through his food. It'll get cold.

She stood and put the baby down and then came and joined him.

The man ate noisily. He ate hungrily and quickly. The first milk had made the potatoes creamy. He scarfed his food and it seemed to loosen something in his chest because between mouthfuls the farmer snorted and coughed and cleared his throat then swallowed whatever it was that his chest was producing. He thumped his sternum to be sure.

When he had cleared his plate the girl was still eating and he said I forgot about the bairn.

The girl spooned some potato into her mouth.

Reckon it could take some milk bread he said. If it's fat enough for the calf it'll be good enough for a bairn.

The girl chewed slowly.

The farmer wiped the back of his hand across his nose then stood and poured more milk from the jug into the same pan and warmed it. He cut some bread and then broke it into the milk. He lifted the pan off the range to cool then poured it into a bowl. He found a spoon and gave it to the girl.

Too late to put it back in the cow anyway he said. Here.

She picked up the baby from the chair and brought it to the table and then carefully spooned the warm milk into its mouth. The baby was sleeping but it stirred to take the liquid. She tried to give it some of the bread but it was unable to chew and regurgitated it.

The farmer half-watched awkwardly with sideways eyes.

The baby took all the milk that the girl could give it. She tried to give it the bread again but it slopped from its mouth.

I'll not be asking what you're doing out in this the man said. And he didn't.

The girl concentrated on the spoon concentrated on the milk concentrated on the baby's mouth.

When the milk was gone she held the baby to her chest and patted its back and then placed it on the chair. She picked up the plates and moved them to the sink but the man said leave them. She went to turn on the tap but he spoke again.

I said leave them.

She sat down.

The farmer stood there for a moment and then he suddenly moved around the kitchen with purpose. He was clumsy. Too big for the cramped room. He shook more coal into the range then pulled the stoppers that fanned the flames and then spoke quietly into the fire.

It's late.

The girl held the back of her fingers to the baby's cheek and then held the baby to her chest and patted its back. Then she unwrapped it from its blankets and saw that it had messed itself.

The man looked over sideways and grimaced.

He went to the scullery where she heard the splashing of water and what she thought was cursing. The man came back and threw her a dirty sheet.

It's from the dog's nest but it'll have to do. There's blankets upstairs.

He hesitated.

You can stop down here by the range where it's warm.

She looked around the room. It was sparse and lacked furniture. A rug covered part of the floor and there was a brown sack in the corner and next to it an axe. The fireplace was blackened and there was a lintel stone above it and there were alcoves in the wall which held empty bottles and a sheep's skull tinged green with damp and the stumps of candles that had dripped wax down onto the floor below. Even with the range glowing it was a cold space. A male's place.

The man turned to her.

Did you hear me?

The girl didn't respond.

Of course you did he said to himself. You're not deaf are you. Dumb as an old yow maybe but not deaf.

He stood and left the room and she heard him walk up the stairs. She could hear his feet moving around.

He came back with a blanket.

Sink's through there.

He threw the blankets to her.

He stared at her and he stared at the baby. There was something about the way he looked at her that she didn't like. She had seen that look worn by another face. It was a look that no man's mask could disguise.

There's scat on it he said.

Bleeding stinks it does he said.

Worse than them pigs he said then stooped to climb the stairs.

He paused halfway up with his back to her and spoke.

I know it's not yours.

2.

WHEN HE RETURNED to the vestry after service he lifted the stole from around his collar folded it and placed it on his desk.

He sat down and smoothed the white surplice that he wore over a black cassock then gently patted his fine red hair down in place. He reached for his hand mirror and checked his reflection then patted it down again.

Tea had been made and left on his desk.

There was a knock at the door.

The Priest lifted the strainer from the pot and poured himself a cup. From his cassock pocket he lifted out a small decorative snuff box whose lid was inset with tortoiseshell and using his fingernail he scooped up a tiny amount of white power from it then tipped it into the tea. He stirred it and tapped the spoon on the edge of the cup.

Come in.

The door opened.

The Priest looked up. His face was pale and the colour of blotting paper. His eyes were rimmed red. Hinckley thought of the pelt of a fox.

He removed his hat.

I'm sorry to disturb you Father.

The calm or disturbance of our mind does not depend so much on what we regard as the more important things of life as in a judicious or injudicious arrangement of the little things of daily occurrence. Do you know who said that?

I'm not familiar Father. I'm sorry.

The thief is sorry that he is to be hanged said the Priest. Not that he is a thief. Uncredited proverb. Origin unknown. What do you want.

I need your help Father.

The Priest lifted his cup and saucer and blew on the tea. He saw a tiny amount of the powder's residue still floating on the surface and felt a small flutter of excitement; a pleasant loosening deep in his bowels. He sipped the tea. There was a quarter segment of lemon on the saucer. He squeezed some juice into the tea then stirred again and blew again.

Sipped again.

Do you.

My bairn's been taken.

The Priest replaced the cup and leaned back in his chair. He resisted the urge to check his hair in the hand mirror again by spreading his hands out on the desk before him. Hinckley saw that his fingernails were abnormally long and manicured. They shone with polish. They were not the fingernails of a man. The Priest caught him staring and he looked away.

By who?

By our help Father. A girl.

What girl?

One of yours.

From St Marys?

Yes.

Which one?

The mute.

The Bulmer girl.

Aye. The dummy.

The Priest said nothing. Something flickered across his eyes. A darkness or a sense of recognition. A rage quelled deep within.

When did this happen?

This morning. In the night.

Which?

In the night.

Tell me how.

She just went. On foot I'd reckon.

17

A hand moved up and reached to the crown of the Priest's head. He slowly ran it down the back gently patting each hair in place then he picked up his tea cup and drank from it slowly. He felt a tightening in his jaw and around his temples. It was the powder demanding attention.

She's not so dumb that she can't get herself a job a bed and a bairn that isn't hers though said the Priest.

Hinckley said nothing.

The Priest stared at him. He breathed in then slowly exhaled. He felt a new sense of sharpness. A cold clean hollowness. He tasted metal.

Hinckley thought he had never seen lips so thin. The Priest's mouth was a gash in his face as if the flesh of his mouth had been pulled tight across his skull then slit with a knife. He wanted to leave the room as soon as he could. He looked away.

There are two things I'll need to know. Why and where.

Hinckley shook his head.

I don't know Father. I don't know where. Most likely she'll have taken to the fells. Anywhere.

She'll have a head start then.

Aye. She could be anywhere.

There are only so many paths out of town and the hunted will always take the easiest exit. That doesn't concern me. What concerns me is why. Why did she take the child.

Hinckley shook his head again.

I wouldn't ask a favour if –

The Priest interrupted him.

You already have.

I'm not one for them normally.

It's not a favour said the Priest.

I know said Hinckley.

It's beyond that.

I'll do whatever it takes. I'll pay.

The Priest snorted and that loosened something within because then he swallowed and said it's not about money. Do you think money is worth anything in the kingdom of heaven? Doesn't a shepherd tend his flock? The girl belongs to me.

And I just want the bairn back said Hinckley. I'll give you owt you want.

Don't let your mouth say anything stupid.

My wife –

Your wife let an imbecile take your child.

It wasn't her fault.

Then it is your fault. It is your skewed judgement that brought you here to rapidly accrue a growing spiritual debt to the church with every passing minute.

Hinckley shook his head in confusion.

If I find the girl or the baby you will be indebted said the Priest. Deeply. Whether the child is dead or alive the debt will stand. If you renege or you disappear or you die the debt carries over.

I'll do whatever I can to help.

It seems like you have done enough.

How do you mean?

The reason.

What?

There's a reason the dummy took your baby said the Priest. You haven't said why. There is always a reason. Did you have her?

Hinckley looked away. He shifted his feet and looked at the tea-pot then wondered if he could smoke in the vestry.

I told you: she's not right. She's built up all wrong.

The Priest smiled for the first time and when he did his thin lips drew back. His gums were large and almost blue in colour but his teeth were small and square. Set deep. Pegged like the milk teeth of children. He raised his tea cup and sipped. Smoothed his hair.

Did you touch her?

Not like that Father. No.

Why did you come to me?

You have the experience and the methods Father said Hinckley.

I am only here to serve my Lord. No-one else.

Yes. I understand.

So.

So.

So whatever happens happens between me and our Lord said the Priest.

He spread his hands on the desk again. Hinckley looked at his nails again. Long and clipped and gleaming like blades.

Are we not after all each and every one of us only answerable to Him?

Yes said Hinckley. I suppose so.

And all you want is the return of your child.

Of course.

Then the lame will leap like a deer and the mute tongue shout for joy said the Priest. Water will gush forth in the wilderness and streams will flow in the desert. I shall find your child Mr Hinckley. And I shall find the girl though in what state I can't say. Whether they are alive or dead is God's will.

Hinckley swallowed then cleared his throat.

Is that the Bible you're quoting Father?

The Priest ignored him.

I'll need help of course.

Will you require transport?

If she has gone on foot then I shall go on foot too said the Priest. The hunter must understand the hunted and follow in their tracks. It's the most efficient way. God provides. The Poacher will be the best man in town for a job of this nature. You'll need to fetch him now. You'll find him in a ditch no doubt. And I'll need a scent of course.

Scent?

Of the child or the girl on a garment. For the dogs.

Hinckley ran a finger along his jawline. He had not yet shaved.

The girl. She has these rags.

Clothes?

No. Like knotted rags. Dirty tatty things they are. She's never without one. She pretends that they are dolls – adopted like. I've caught her whispering to them. Silent whispers of course. Her mouth going but no words coming like.

The Priest drained the last of his tea.

A rag will be fine. And something from the child. Anything.

Margaret could find something. These dogs –

You should go said the Priest. Get the Poacher. Tell him what you told me.

What if he won't come? He's a selfish bastard.

Tell him he'll be exonerated of all outstanding charges. He will be formally pardoned for past misdemeanours rewarded handsomely by the Church and looked upon favourably by our Father. And if he still won't come tell him I'll be paying him a visit when he least expects it.

Yes.

Go said the Priest. Now.

Hinckley turned away. The Priest tipped his head back and drained his cup.

WHEN SHE STIRRED again the fire had died down but the range was glowing.

The baby was asleep on one of the other chairs. It had woken once but the girl had rocked it back and forth and now it was asleep again; a tiny bundle bathed in an orange glow. Outside a strong wind whistled around the sharp corners of the house.

And the man was standing there looking at her. A breathing shadow. She could smell him. Sweat and soil and silage.

She recognised it; it was the smell of the bogs and animal pens. It was the smell of farming. It was the smell of her father;

the one before the one who called himself that. His face she could not remember though she still recalled his boots and his breath and the way his big hands gripped her thin arms – and his smell. Definitely the smell. The girl realised after all these years that she still remembered the wet dog scent of the fell tops hanging from him. All the liquids of the world stirred together and dried down to the stain of him.

She closed her eyes again to wish the farmer away – to wish the memory of her father away – but when she had counted to ten he was still there his breathing long and deep and laboured as if he had just come in from the fell.

There was something wrong with the atmosphere of the room. The air was disturbed. She sensed a movement from him. His arm moving one way and then another. And then she thought she heard him sigh but she wasn't sure.

She could smell him as he moved closer through the half-light. She felt coiled and cornered.

He moved towards her and reached out his hand and his eyes were stone and then his hand was on her sliding beneath her to grab at a breast and then he was massaging it and breathing heavily and the glow of the coals turned the room from dark orange to carmine.

She felt his thick dry fingers tugging and nipping at her tight skin and her breast hurt and her chest hurt and she didn't dare draw breath but then suddenly he was drawing back and cursing. His hand rose up in front of his face and he sniffed his fingers and it was at that moment that she felt the spreading wetness of the lactation from her nipple. A milky mess; her own surrogate beastings. It was a miracle. It had to be.

God providing. God in action.

I have fed you with milk and not with meat she thought. *For hitherto ye were not able to bear it; neither yet now are ye able.*

The man turned and left and stumbled on the stairs.

She stood and checked on the baby. It was sleeping soundly its eyelids fluttering and its mouth clucking and chomping and working away on an imaginary teat. She uncovered her breast and leaned to it.

THE FARMER WAS UP before it was light.

He came and went and then he came again. The baby had soiled itself again so the girl took it out of the dog's blanket and washed around its crotch and then found her blankets. They had been hung above the range and were warm and brittle to the touch.

The man came in with coal and logs. It wasn't raining.

He didn't say anything. Didn't look at her. He folded more kindling into the range and worked the stoppers until the wood took.

He had his back to her and didn't look at her once.

I'll do us a bowl of hasty he said. Then you'll be gone.

He took a small sack of wheat flour and scooped some into a pan then added milk a fistful of oats and a pinch of salt. He set it down then made some tea.

The baby gurgled and a bubble formed on its lips.

They ate in silence: the girl in the chair and the farmer standing at the bench by the range and looking out the mullion windows into the yard where the sky had cleared. When he had finished he put his bowl on the bench then he came to the girl and picked up her bowl of hasty pudding even though she was still eating it.

She still held the spoon in her hand.

He stood in front of her just as he had in the early hours. He loomed over her and looked down with disdain. His eyes put a shiver through her. She saw for the first time that that they were as grey as the slate and the scree and the Cumbrian cairns that scratched at the sky.

I know what you are he said quietly. She looked down into her lap.

You're a dummy.

As he said this his lips curled back into a sneer.

A dummy and a big lump of a heifer that's good for nowt but milking.

She pressed herself straight against the back of the chair. She could smell him again. Strong and stale. It hung from him. Framed him. She couldn't breathe.

He looked down to her chest then back up then sneered again. His mouth a slit in his face.

Thought my luck had turned when you fetched up.

He snorted.

Fat chance.

He looked into her eyes and she held her breath.

Just my luck to get a dummy. And a sow of a dummy at that.

He leaned down and she arched her back but then he straightened and pointed out to the yard.

Go he said.

Now he said.

Before I change me mind he said.

THE POACHER ARRIVED unshaven and unsteady in a long oilskin mac that gave off a strong waxy stench. Rank. His accent was thick the vowels swollen and cumbersome in his slack mouth. His eyes glassy. The Priest did not rise from his chair.

May I remind you where you are.

Father?

You are in a place of worship. Your hat. Remove it.

The Poacher lifted his cap and folded it into his pocket then ran his fingers through his thick dark hair. It stood like the hackles of a fell terrier that's cornered a fox.

Hinckley sent us.

He's told you of his dilemma.

The Poacher shrugged.

So you know time is of the essence said the Priest.

I don't know nothing said the Poacher.

The Priest raised an eyebrow.

I don't know nowt Father said the Poacher.

Your tracking and hunting skills are required immediately as is your knowledge of the fells.

Aye well. I gathered that. Tommo Hinckley said summat about payment.

You'll be paid.

And me record.

Your record will be cleared.

How's that like.

The Church has a lot of friends in town. I'm sure you know that. Clout. I'll make sure of it.

What are we hunting anyway asked the Poacher.

Not what. Who.

Who?

Yes.

A person?

Yes. A girl.

We're hunting a lass?

Yes. A young girl who has absconded with a child.

What's absconded?

Run away.

With her bairn.

Not her child – no. Someone else's.

Whose?

Hinckley's.

He never even said. He's a miserable bugger him.

He's more miserable now said the Priest.

I didn't know he had a bairn said the Poacher.

He might not for much longer.

Didn't think his missus was capable.

That's their business said the Priest.

Who's this girl?

One of the fold.

One of your St Mary's lot?

If you mean one of the young ladies from the orphanage then yes. One of the blighted.

What's blighted? Like in potatoes?

Never mind.

What's the family name? the Poacher asked.

What does it matter. She's my responsibility.

Not much. Just making conversation.

I don't need you for your conversational skills.

The Poacher paused. A minute passed.

Well where's she got to he said.

That's for us to find out said the Priest. Hinckley thinks the fells most likely. And so do I.

How will we find her?

With your knowledge said the Priest.

Knowledge. I like that. Rare's the time anyone says I've got me some knowledge especially a man of the cloth like yourself.

With God's guidance we'll prevail.

And our Perses.

Who's Perses?

Me hound. Named after some old God. He'll sniff her out.

I'm aware of who Perses is. The God of Destruction.

Aye. That sounds about right.

You don't strike me as a scholar of the classics.

I'm not a scholar of nothing but snaring and trapping Father. I'm no book learner. Bad for your eyesight and a lot more besides. No. This one was already named when I got him from a gadgie over Threlkeld way at eight week old. Rum type he was. Up from the city and fancied his chances with a farm. I gave him two year; he lasted less than one.

Then as an afterthought the Poacher said: they reckoned folk kept lifting his sheep.

How long before you can gather your dog and some provisions?

Don't need no provisions.

We don't know how long we'll be gone.

She'll have not got far. We'll find her by tea time.

I admire your optimism.

I'm a glass half full fella me.

Strange. Because from here you smell like a glass entirely empty man.

The Poacher stiffened.

That's as maybe. But nature's my larder. I'll just need a sit down for a little while first.

There's no time for that.

I just need to check my eyelids for holes Father.

I'm assuming you've been drinking.

It's a fair assumption.

How long for?

Well now. I started young so reckon it must be twenty-five year.

I mean how long this time.

Couple or three days. Don't fully remember. Depends what day it is today.

You look a state said the Priest.

I always look like this.

I hope you're not going to be a hindrance.

I said I'd help said the Poacher. And I will.

I don't believe you did.

I'm saying it now.

Fine said the Priest. Then get your dog and meet me here in an hour.

An hour?

One hour.

Have I got time to –

No.

THE PRIEST HAD finished packing a bag and changed into a tweed overcoat when there was a scratching at the door.

He opened it to the Poacher and a dog straining on its lead so hard that it was standing on its two back legs with its front legs pawing at the space where the door had been. It was nearly as tall as the Priest. Flecks of foam gathered at the corners of its mouth.

You're late.

Aye well said the Poacher. Like I said I've not had much kip this week.

Well you better get used to it. We've got a walk ahead of us.

Had to eat some duck eggs said the Poacher as he was pulled into the vestry by the dog. He was still unshaven and had not changed his clothes.

This here's Perses. A bull mastiff. You've got old English bulldog mixed in with English mastiff. Call it the Gamekeeper's Night Dog; bred for seeing off poachers like me they are. That's why I've got him. To keep one step ahead in the game like. Know your enemy and that. Not that he comes with us everywhere. Can't be scaring the creatures off else there'd be nothing left for my pantry.

Did Hinckley give you something for the scent?

Aye he gave us these.

The Poacher pulled a clutch of rags from his pocket and rubbed them in the dog's face.

He's not much used to the indoors is Persey.

Then we should get going. Where is your bag?

You just worry about yourself Father. You're looking pale if you don't mind my saying.

I do. I do mind.

Sorry.

Don't be sorry. Just do what you're here to do. Help me find the girl.

WHEN THE FARM dwellings had long disappeared behind her the girl crouched down behind a wall and rested a while.

She unwrapped the baby and lifted it out from its blanket and removed the corner wedge of ham from beneath its back that she had torn from one of the cured sides hanging in the scullery and the large potato that had been by the baby's feet. It felt heavy in her hand. She put it in her pocket along with the meat and a spoon that she had also slipped up her sleeve. The farmer's debt.

As she held the baby in front of her it emitted a stream of urine. She tried to move out of the way but some of it caught her hand and she was surprised by how warm it felt. Hot even. It was golden. The baby was thirsty. Short on fluids. Draining remnants.

She wiped her hand off on the grass then wrapped the child back up in its blankets.

She had a sheet too. She'd taken it from the farmer's clothes line.

He must have hung it first thing and now she was folding it and fashioning it to form a crude pouch with which to hold the child tight across her back. The first attempt failed as the baby squirmed and she couldn't tie the knot right. She tried again by lying the bairn on the sheet on the ground and then leaning back on it to make sure it was held flat against her with its legs spread-eagled then she tied the sheet tighter this time with a front knot down by her left hip. Then she slowly stood. The baby was held firm across her back now.

The girl leaned against the dry stone wall for a moment and then started walking again. It felt much easier. The weight was more evenly spread and her broad hips and legs shared some of the burden and her hands were free. She felt less vulnerable walking across uneven ground where rocks lurked in the long grass.

The baby gurgled in her ear. It wore the same clothes she had taken it in; the clothes Hinckley's wages had bought.

He had answered shirtless that very first day down in the town. Her memory of him would always be of that first moment: his white chest concave and not at all fleshy and rounded like hers. He had been in the middle of washing himself and had a towel rolled around his neck. She could see his ribs and the wisp of hair at the centre of his chest and around two tiny nipples. His belly button was an ugly nub. The stump of something cut and cauterized.

Sister had gasped and a hand fluttered to her mouth and then she regained herself.

Mr Hinckley.

Aye.

We've come from St Mary's.

Eh?

St Mary's.

Is it the wife you're wanting?

It's about the girl.

Sister had her by the elbow again. Her case at her feet.

The girl had looked at the man's bare torso. The man looked from Sister to the girl then back again.

Eh?

She's the help.

Hold on a minute.

He turned and went back into the house and the door gently closed itself behind him. Sister tutted and ran a finger around the rim of her tight collar.

Stop slouching she hissed even though the girl wasn't.

Then she muttered something to herself. A piece of scripture: the turning away of the simple shall slay them and the prosperity of fools shall destroy them she said.

She was always doing that was Sister. Muttering quotes from The Book. She had ones for every occasion. The girls were encouraged to do the same. They were drilled into them. Taught by rote as most could not read.

The man returned wearing a shirt this time but still open at the chest. The girl noticed shaving soap on the lobe of one of his ears. She looked at his Adam's apple bulbous in his taut lathered throat. Those ridiculous nipples dark and flat and tiny.

What is it you're after?

It has been arranged for you to receive some help about the place Mr. Hinckley. From the girl. I believe your wife is sick.

She's sick alright. Coughing up the black stuff half the night. And there's the wean to look after an all. It might be that she mentioned it a couple or three weeks back. I can't say it all goes in. She's asleep now but.

Sister didn't say anything to this.

This is the lass then he said.

Yes.

The man wiped the foam from his ear and considered the girl.

Well what's she got to say for herself.

Nothing.

Nothing?

She's the silent type.

Well what's that supposed to mean?

She's a mute said the Sister her hand still at the girl's elbow. Never speaks a word.

The man stared at the girl until he broke her gaze and she looked away.

She'll hear you alright though said Sister. She might act like she's not heard you but she will have. It gets through eventually.

Well what's wrong with her the man asked as the girl watched his scrawny throat pulse and bulge like that of a chicken on a block then she looked past him into the darkness of the terraced house. I bet I could make her talk. Here – watch.

He leaned over with his hands on his thighs.

Go on then girl – say summat. There's a present for you if you do.

She pursed her lips and said nothing.

Go on. Just give us a word.

She looked away.

One word. Even a squeak.

She's tapped said Sister. Bad breeding is what has done it. Bad breeding and a families' devilish ways. You'll not get a peep out of her. Trust me. I doubt she could form a sentence even if her mouth let her.

He shook his head.

I'll get a word out of her. You just give me time.

Well said Sister. She's a good little worker I'll give her that.

She's not that little. Bet she eats a lot.

Just enough to get by.

Hinckley sniffed.

Diseases?

None that we know about.

What about law breaking? I'll not tolerate thieving.

No. She's been with us since she was a wean. Brought up the Godly way. The right way.

Aye well said Hinckley.

She might not read or write but she can cook and clean and scrub like no-one. She could recite the scriptures if she had a tongue in her head. She's had years of practice. Builds a good fire too.

If she's so handy about the place he said why is it you're wanting rid of her?

She's come of age Mr Hinckley. They cannot stay forever. None of them. We need the beds. Your wife said it would be agreeable. Said she'd be a help with the young one.

Aye. Didn't know it was today though.

He looked at the girl's face again.

She's helped raise some of the babies that have come through said the Sister. She's trained in the ways. Weaning and washing feeding and fetching. All of that.

Hinckley had said nothing.

And she's Christianly said the Sister.

He nodded.

Aye you said. Another thing I cannot abide is noise me. Specially in the mornings. So she's got that in her favour. Don't know if I can feed another mouth though what with the bairn.

I understand. That is why St Mary's is happy to provide a small stipend.

He sniffed again then gently ran his finger over his flat stomach idly rubbing it.

Is that right?

Yes though of course the greater reward comes from up above.

Aye said the man. Up above.

The reward is great in heaven.

What's the family name?

Bulmer.

I don't believe I know it.

You'd be best not to said Sister. Rum lot. Bad breeding if you know what I mean.

From the town?

Up top. One of the farms.

The girl felt for her dolly rag in her pocket and squeezed it.

Which one? I've done a bit of work up there. Walling and that.

I don't know Mr Hinckley. She came to St Mary's a long time ago. She is our longest standing resident.

Why?

Why?

Aye – why did she come to you? Must have been something up.

I believe there were some problems at home.

What problems.

I don't know. Impropriety. Her people were incapable.

I bet they were. What do they call her?

Isabelle. Bell.

Isabelle Bell?

Isabelle. Bell for short.

The man touched his face again.

Well she could do with some help could Margaret what with all her coughing. No doubt about that – the amount of nappies the bairn gets through. And there's the housework. She'd have to go in the nursery though. On the floor like.

You wouldn't mind that said the Sister. Would you?

She squeezed the girl's elbow. The girl flinched and pulled her arm away. Sister took it again and held it harder and tighter than ever.

She'd be grateful of any roof Mr Hinckley. A roof and food and a floor and a good day's work. That's all she needs. He will provide the rest.

Who will?

He will Mr Hinckley.

Oh aye. Him.

Like I said neither you or your wife should have any problems out of this one. She's stubborn when she wants to be alright and she's on the shelf for good but she's not like some of the others with their cursing and their carousing and their wickedness. She's well disciplined and if she steps out of line you be sure to let me or the Father know about it.

Oh Hinckley said and then scrutinised the girl with renewed interest. One of Father's girls is she?

Sister nodded. She ran her finger around her collar again.

And this stipend he said.

It's a monthly payment – in cash. Modest but it'll help with food and fuel. A false balance is an abomination to the Lord but a just weight is His delight.

Well then.

A hand was at the girl's back again. Sister's hand. It gave a push. The girl stepped forward. She was close to the man. She could smell cigarettes on him. Cigarettes and shaving. Behind him the house smelled of boiled onions and sweat. Milk on the turn.

You best come in then he said.

The girl hadn't moved. Couldn't move. He stepped aside. Sister shoved her forward. She stumbled and fell into the house. Sister slid her suitcase in behind her.

Hinckley closed the door.

THE DOG PICKED up the scent at the end of Hinckley's street and took them to the nearest mud track out of town. It was an obscure grassy rut that rose sharply up the hill that sat behind the town hall and which lead to the lower slopes of the Eastern fells.

The Priest let the animal take the lead. He noticed the Poacher dragging his foot.

After nearly two hours of walking the Poacher stopped and urinated where he stood.

They were high along the ridge of the valley.

We're on the right track Father he said without turning round. Persey as good as says so. He's pulled us along all the way. We'll find this girl of yours in no time. Mark my words.

You're limping said the Priest. Are you tired already?

Nope.

The Poacher shook himself off then reached into a pocket and pulled out a greaseproof parcel. The paper was soaked through with oil. He opened it and broke off a piece of flapjack. He wedged it into his cheek. Then as an afterthought he offered the open parcel to the Priest.

He shook his head.

Suit yourself.

The Poacher threw a scrap to the dog then folded the parcel away. He untied the rope from the dog's neck and let it roam free. It wandered away and then squatted. It bent double – a crude question mark against the landscape. The Priest smelled its evacuation on the breeze.

What'll you do when you find her said the Poacher.

I'll return the child.

What about the girl?

The Priest shrugged.

I thought you said she belonged to you.

She belongs to God said the Priest. And I am an envoy of God. It's His will. He'll decide her fate.

How will you know?

How will I know what?

What that fate is said the Poacher.

Because that eventuality will reveal itself in time.

What if she's harmed the bairn though.

It's God's judgement.

And you believe all that do you Father?

All that.

Fate and God's will. All that stuff.

All that stuff is the foundation of my belief system and the core of my existence. Yes of course I believe that.

And you believe that God controls everything.

That's a very simple way of seeing it said the Priest. But yes in a manner of speaking.

And He made all this. The mountains and valleys.

The Ice Age made the mountains and valleys.

So not God.

God froze the water to make the glaciers then God melted the glaciers that made the mountains and valleys.

And that's in The Bible.

No it's not in The Bible said the Priest.

So how do you know?

How do I know.

Yes.

How does one know anything said the Priest. I know because I believe in Him. I place my faith in Him and I know that His guidance is all I need. Every decision I make is with His hand on my shoulder. Jesus said if you have faith and don't doubt then you can even say to a mountain may God lift you up and throw you into the sea and it will happen. We should carry on walking. Look – the dog is getting ahead of us.

Now that I'd like to see.

The Priest's face was tight with impatience.

What? he said.

Can you lift mountains Father?

Don't be idiotic.

Could Jesus?

Jesus was a humble man.

So it's God who can throw mountains into the sea.

If you like.

The Poacher paused.

I'm not sure I believe that he said.

Have you ever seen a rock fall? A landslide?

No Father.

But you've seen evidence of them. You believe them to be true.

No reason not to.

And you've heard of earthquakes.

Not round these parts.

But you've heard of them.

Yes. In other lands.

And volcanoes. And great tidal waves.

Yes.

You've heard of Pompeii.

Don't believe I have.

But you accept as fact that oak trees grow from acorns.

Everyone knows that.

Well then. That's God's capability.

The Poacher fell silent and they continued to climb. After a few minutes he spoke again.

Is it true what they say about you Father?

It depends who they are and what they say.

Around the town like.

How could I possibly know what they say.

That there's more to you than meets the eye said the Poacher.

I hope so.

There are stories Father.

I'm sure there are.

Scandalous stuff. I'm sure it's all lies. Hearsay like.

Well I can't refute them if you don't share them.

I'm not sure I could repeat them Father.

Well shut up and keep walking.

Some of the people said the Poacher with caution. They're scared of you.

Then they can't be believers. Because believers do not fear. The people in my congregation do not feel fear. Or if any do it is a fear of God weighing judgment on them for their secret sins. Nothing more. Mainly though they know only the love of Jesus Christ.

Is that right.

Yes.

So as a believer you're not afraid of owt.

No said the Priest. Nothing.

Nothing?

Nothing.

Maybe it is true what they say then said the Poacher.

And that is?

I'm not sure I can say Father. Ungodly things.

Then stop talking and keep walking. We're wasting time.

3.

THOUGH OF A similar colour the shape of the tent distinguished it from the landscape around it. It looked like a fallen kite or turf cut from the fell side; abstract yet man-made. Clean lines.

As she got closer the girl saw that it was a green canvas dwelling whose sagging sides were moving. They were being prodded from within. Before she could turn and walk the long way around first a hand and then a head appeared from the opening at the front. The hand was holding a small pan. The body of a man followed it and unfolded itself from the knees upwards then stretched and yawned.

There was nowhere for the girl to hide; no point in ducking. She froze. Held the bairn tight. The man looked around and saw her and waved.

The man turned to the flap at the front of the tent and said something.

Another head appeared. A woman this time. Prone and sleep-tousled. Middle aged.

She looked first left and then right to where the girl stood and who she now silently surveyed.

The women said something quietly to the man who also considered the girl for a moment. He was short and bald and almost perfectly circular. He lifted his pan.

Libation?

The woman retracted into the tent as the man reached in and pulled out a water container and a metal device. A canister of some sort. He put the device on the ground and unfolded some metal spokes from it which locked into place then he turned a button near the bottom and fumbled for some matches. He lit one and a flame ignited. The flame was blue and unlike any the girl had ever seen.

He poured water into the pan and set it on the flame.

The world's first soot-free stove.

He said this to the girl in a loud voice that seemed to carry right across the valley. He smiled.

Not literally the very first of course but certainly a rarity he continued. I bet you've never seen one before. Come and have a look if you like. It's based on the same design principle as a blowtorch.

The man paused and studied the girl's face for a response. When he spoke again it was even louder than before.

Only it blows *upwards* instead of outwards. Runs on kerosene – which can be a bugger to find out here.

The girl flinched at language that seemed peculiar when spoken in an accent that was crisp and clear and authoritative. It was a voice that had never known doubt or uncertainty. He was not from these valleys. She took some steps towards him. It was all the encouragement he needed to continue.

Upward instead of outwards he said again. It's really very simple.

Stop shouting Donald said the woman from the tent. Unless she's deaf she can hear you well enough without you shouting.

As you can see we have a brass fuel tank at the base the fat man continued without lowering his volume. The rising tube leads through the vapour nozzle to what we call a spirit cup. This sits beneath the reinforced steel top grill. The fuel sits in the spirit cup ready for ignition. As is evident three simple legs support it below. It measures eight and one half inches in height and seven inches in diameter. It weighs no more than two and one half pounds. Your child could carry it on its back if so inclined.

Don't be *ridiculous* Donald said the voice from the tent again.

The girl saw that small bubbles were rising in the pan.

Design genius he said. It holds two pints of kerosene which when ignited can produce a continuous flame for four hours. That's a lot of hot drinks.

The man squatted and examined the device.

Yes he continued. This pressurised hand-pump is what differentiates it from other less successful designs which have flooded the market of late. Because you see the hand-pump then forces the fuel through the entire mechanism to emit a light spray which mixes with the air to form what you can see here: a beautiful blue flame that burns without soot or smoke. When turned this tiny hand screw can even adjust the height of the flames. No wick. No oil. Amazing. Works in all weathers.

The water in the pan was roiling now and the man turned to reach into the tent for something but the woman blocked his path as she came out from under the canvas on her hands and knees with a green blanket wrapped around her shoulders.

Ignore him she said to the girl.

She did not seem happy.

Designed by a Swiss chap said the man.

We've barely any food said the woman. We can't feed you if that's what you're after.

Call it a Primus.

The girl looked from the woman to the man to the stove. The woman stood. She was tall and thin and had eyes like spent matches and an inverted mouth that could never smile. She thought of the rear of a cat. The woman's height made the man seem even shorter and rounder. Both were wearing stout boots and thick woollen trousers tucked into socks. Together they were a comically ill-matched coupling.

We've to go into the village to get supplies said the woman.

For the big trip said the man.

For my breakfast.

They both looked at the girl but when she didn't respond the man said: Helvellyn you see. We're walking over to Ullswater way. Could be ten or twenty miles yet. We'll have a night on the shores at Glenridding and then shall head up the Grisedale valley to ascend the most celestial mountain in the whole of the Lakelands –

That's what he thinks the woman sniffed.

– that great stone cathedral that inspired the bard of the north Mr William Wordsworth himself to write of – and I quote – an inmate of a mountain-dwelling thou hast climb aloft and gazed. From the watch-towers of Helvellyn; awed delighted and amazed.

I'm hungry Donald said the woman.

She adjusted the blanket around her shoulders.

A record of commotion the man gasped lost in his recital. Which a thousand ridges yield. Ridge and gulf and distant ocean. Gleaming like a silver shield.

I'm not going another day eating nothing but your damned dried berry simnel cake said his companion. I told you: get your house in order or I'm turning back today. You're forever drunk on these damned heroic notions of yours; always out to prove your shrinking sense of manhood. Climbing some windy bluff in a godforsaken backwater is not my idea of a holiday. This is the last time Donald. The very last time.

The girl shrank inside herself waiting for the inevitable explosion of violence from the man at this but it never came. Not so much as a slap or a pinch. No hair-dragging or flesh twisting. The man offered nothing in the way of punishment. It was as if they were equal. No – it was as if her words held some sort of power over him.

Instead he ignored the woman and spoke with an increasing sense of theatricality. His arms rose up in front of him and then opened out as if he were addressing the entire fell:

How glorious it is to pitch one's temporary dwelling exactly where one pleases he said. Yes – maiden! Now take flight – inherit. Alps or Andes – they are thine. With the morning's roseate spirits sweep their length of snowy line.

The girl looked at the woman looking at her husband with contempt. She spoke through her thin lips.

Not this again. You're not on Shaftesbury Avenue now.

The woman turned to partly address the girl but they both knew it was to her husband that she was really speaking.

He's dreaming of a standing ovation she muttered. That would be a first. There's a joke that circulates about him: never a dry eye in the house when this one takes the stage. Because they're all shut. Asleep. Dreaming of better places.

Still in a reverie of sorts the man ignored the criticism and addressed the girl.

We hope to see the spot where that great symbol of Romanticism poor Charles Gough perished on the mountain he continued oblivious. Fell off the arête known as Striding Edge during a solo climb over to Grasmere. He should have employed a guide of course but that just wasn't his way. Not old Goughy. A distant relative of mine you know.

The water is boiling said the woman but the man pressed on with his soliloquy.

Yes my father had one of his paintings hanging in the Southwold house. And do you know the most remarkable thing is they say his loyal dog Foxie watched over his body for three whole months until they found him. Amazing. Of this heroic pairing of man and beast it was Scott who wrote: faithful in death – his mute favourite attended – the much-loved remains of her master defended.

What the silly Scotsman neglected to mention was that his loyal dog Foxie ate the flesh right off his bones the woman said dismissively. Come spring they found nothing but his skeleton and his broken spectacles. At least the dog was a practical thinker where his master surely was not.

Foxie had a pup up there though said the man.

Which died she snapped. The water's boiling Donald for heaven's sake.

And it was. The stove was working and the water was bubbling up to the rim and then it was curling over the edge but the man was lost in his thoughts of heroic Charles Gough prone and perishing on the shale shore of Red Tarn. Then the water was hissing into the flame and extinguishing it and the hiss of the gas and the sizzle of the evaporating water blended into one and only then did the short bald man break from his Romantic trance and turn back to the object of his affection – his new soot-free stove.

Blast it he said. He crouched to lift the pan off but the handle was hot and it seared his hand. The girl heard it imprint a line across his palm. He leapt backwards and dropped it then shook his hand as if it were on fire.

Oh blast it just...blast it.

Idiot said his wife. You literally cannot even boil a pan of water.

The woman began to beat the man about the head with her hand.

Unnoticed the girl left the couple bickering on the hillside in their wool knitwear as a breeze took up and lifted the flap of their canvas dwelling.

SHE STUDIED THE sky and saw that although it was cloudy the nebulous trails were low and scudding across at speed as if it were the sky that was turning and not the earth.

If there was to be rain it wouldn't stay fixed. The rain would move and so would she.

All this activity overhead bolstered the girl's energy and she dug in determining a fresh resolve to put as much space between herself and the farmer as possible. Soon he might notice the missing meat and the spoon and the sheet or worse – he might report her. A lass with a bairn and something not right.

Walking was easier. She moved quickly and began to feel a warmth in her clothes as her back dampened with sweat beneath the baby. She pictured a beach and beyond the beach water and then beyond the horizon an island with apple trees and pear trees and chickens and pigs and no people.

Once they reached the water they would cross it. Or maybe it would part for them. Probably this would happen. The test would be to get to the sea and then He would do the rest for doesn't He say *lift up your staff and stretch out your hand over the sea and divide it that the people of Israel may go through the sea on dry ground.*

There they would walk on over dry rocks and amongst flapping sea creatures until they reached the island that looked most like the one in her head and they would make it theirs. And so the waters would close behind them. And so they would be free. It seemed so real she knew it must be out there. With His guidance.

She walked for an hour and then another hour.

The baby dozed and then it awoke and plucked and tugged at her earlobe and twisted its fingers in her hair.

She was following a path that ran alongside some grazing fields in the lowlands. The meadow slowly rose upwards towards a sky that had cleared to a deep blue. She fixed her eyes on a copse and headed towards it. Beyond that she could see the hazy outline of mountains; layer upon layer of fading shapes silently stacked. From here they looked impenetrable. Imprisoning.

When she reached the trees the girl followed a shallow slow-moving chalk runnel a way in then when she felt she was far enough out of sight she stopped and unwrapped the baby.

The child looked pale and bloodless but it lay on its back and kicked its legs and tried to grab fistfuls of the space above it. She knelt and took a long drink from the stream. She washed her face and neck and hands and then sat the baby up and cupped and spooned some of the stream into its mouth. This seemed to enliven the child.

It was cool and still in the trees and the way the light came down in shafts through the lattice of branches was like being in a church. It felt like a hallowed space in there and the way the sun illuminated patches of the copse's floor reminded her of a stained glass window and she didn't want to break the silence by moving or even breathing. She inhaled until the church became a copse again and the sweat on her back dried and became a cold metal disc.

The runnel was no more than a foot across and six inches deep – a river in miniature. She lay on her side by it and watched the flow carry leaves and bugs and she imagined that it was a great torrent. She knew that she may have to cross such a river and for a moment the thought of her powerless against nature scared the girl.

She sat and pulled blades from her hair then took the piece of ham from her pocket and tore a strip off and chewed it slowly. It was salted and smoked and delicious and she ate some more.

She chewed a smaller piece and mixed it with her saliva until it was a pink mush in her mouth then she put it on the spoon and tilted it into the baby's mouth who it took it hungrily and swallowed it straight down. She did it again. Once twice then again. She did exactly what she had seen nesting birds do with their young. As good a guide as any.

Colour returned to the baby's cheeks and the girl gave it some more water then took another long drink herself and then lay back in the grass and dozed – dirt scalped and skin scratched. Tremble spent and nightmare haunted.

THERE HAD BEEN mice under the nursery floorboards and walls. The girl heard them that first night and every night afterwards – skittering and scratching in the early hours always when the house was still and the silence amplified their movements.

They sounded like nails scratching at the inside of closed coffin lids. That's what she saw when she heard them: the final frantic moments of the buried living.

Such things used to happen. One of the Sisters had told her so.

Once the mice had woken her just before dawn each morning the girl lay on her side shivering under her blanket and waited until the baby started babbling. Then she stood and the skirting boards and walls were silent and it was as if she had imagined the incessant insistent scratching. A house awaiting death or something as hugely significant. That's what that place had been.

She focused on the baby because the baby was lightness. The baby was magic.

The baby was hope.

It loved the girl and the girl loved it as if it were her own and soon she formed a routine that only strengthened that bond.

Hinckley's wife with her permanent exhaustion and worsening cough was too ill to show the child any attention. She spent the day with her head turned away and rising only to do her ablutions. The girl suspected she cared for her child no more than she did for her brooding uninterested husband.

But the girl. The girl the child liked. The bond grew until her breasts started to swell and her stomach stirred with new feelings and she could taste bitter new flavours in her mouth. They were not unpleasant just different. Unexpected.

She took to sleeping with the child curled up next to her on the nursery floor – the child pressed into the pit of her arm – and when it awoke and cried she didn't mind because the bond had strengthened further still and when its mother showed disdain she made sure to take the baby to the nursery and to shower it in kisses and when the father turned up dusty and tired or drunk and angry she made sure she stood between him and the baby so that no harm might come of it. Better her than the baby.

And the more time she spent with the child the less the girl had thoughts about St. Mary's and the Sisters and everything that had happened there; things so unspeakable that they blurred with her nightmares to form a painful unreality in which she had begun to live almost permanently. Those nocturnal awakenings. Father at her like that. Under the blankets and up the shirt. Pawing and tearing so sleep could only ever be a broken thing that kept her in a perpetual state of fatigue and confusion when day-time dozing was considered sinful and punishable by another visit from Father. So it had gone. And for this she was expected to be grateful.

Think of your poor siblings next time you're shedding those tears said the Sisters. Up there with those un-Godly beasts. Those wicked wicked people. No. You were the lucky one girl. Silence is virtuous and anyway don't your ears work alright? He said faith comes from hearing and hearing through the word of Christ. Give thanks to the Lord for His steadfast love endures forever.

Though the past lived on in nightmares she tried not to think on these matters any more. Her new chores didn't allow for reflection. The grate had to be emptied and cleaned and the ashes disposed of and then the hearth swept. Then the fire was to be built and lit and the same in the kitchen. It was her job to keep them going. This she did sleepily – her forearms aching from the buckets of coal she had to fetch in.

Then there was Hinckley's tea and his eggs and his toast to have ready before seven and his bait box prepared for when he left. Bread and cheese and boiled eggs and anything else left over from the night before.

There were logs that needed splitting. There were always logs that needed splitting. Lifting and hefting. Gathering.

Those late spring mornings when Hinckley started work early he had her doing all of these chores before he was up and washed and dressed and at the table to eat in silence.

Which suited her.

It is good that one should wait quietly for the salvation of the Lord.

The mornings were light and she tried not to think of winter – of the dark days ahead and the cold water washes and the frosted fractals on the windows. Just like at St Mary's. St Mary's she tried to forget about. She was here now and at least Hinckley wasn't on her like Father had been. There were no other girls either and for this she was thankful. For the girls in St Mary's were broken and if they weren't then that changed soon enough. Father and the Sisters saw to that. Friendships were not encouraged either as they detracted from attention to Him. Friendships encouraged camaraderie which led to dissent.

And there was the baby now.

The baby just about made it worth it.

When she washed and changed it it began to grip the girl's finger and when she made a dolly rag out of an old bit of cloth and dangled it over the cot its eyes opened wide and it smiled and gurgled.

Mrs Hinckley was in her bed most days – nerves they said – and when her husband was gone the girl would put a blanket down in front of the range and she and the child would roll and wrestle there on the floor and she would tickle it until it urinated with excitement then she would clean it and dress it and start again.

Only on her good days would Mrs Hinckley take the child in her room – on her bed – and even then only for half an hour or so because after that she would be exhausted and she'd ask the girl to take the child and close the door behind her and later she'd not even be able to eat for the fatigue.

The afternoons were the best. In the afternoons the bairn got sleepy and the girl would take a break from her chores and move a chair to the front door and she would sit there on the step and watch the sky and look up at the mountains and people would walk by and nod their heads. Or she would go to the nursery window from which she could see the lake if she opened it wide and leaned out far enough.

Soon the mountains were already green with dense summer foliage and where they weren't green they were grey with rock falls and protruding crags because the fells were pitted with the signs of industry too: from the holes hewn by Neolithic clans making axe heads to trade around the country through to the dynamite-blasted quarries and mines dug in the pursuit of slate gypsum and graphite. Then beyond these fells into further valleys the mining of lead and copper and zinc and barite and haematite and tungsten too. Up there on the fells there was still evidence of old lime kilns; the dwellings of those that tended them now little more that ramshackle heaps of fallen rock.

Hinckley worked with stone. A mason. Walling and paving and fireplaces mainly. He was on a team that would get sent out with chisels and mallets to wherever the work was. Most of it was around the town or the hamlets that skirted the fringes because beyond it there was nothing but fells and hills for miles around and the farmsteads were too poor to need much doing. Town was where the money was. Occasionally he did gravestones on the side. His calligraphy was revered his hand steady. He made a wage. Just enough for the house and food and the coal man. Clothes for the child. Medicine for the wife. Beer sometimes. He took it when he could afford it – and when he took it it was to excess.

Two Saturdays after the girl arrived and a routine had been established he fetched up drunk and back-handed her when she brought him burnt dropped scones. After that he lurched upstairs and the girl heard the bed creaking and the sound of Mrs Hinckley coughing and groaning. Her face burned.

The wine of violence...the poison of serpents. The cruel venom of asps.

The following morning he said nothing to the girl. Just ate his eggs in silence and ignored the cries of his child.

WHEN SHE AWOKE she didn't know how much time had passed but the trees looked the same and the sky looked the same and the baby was still trying to grab the space in front of its face with its small curled fingers so she sat up. The girl played with the baby for a few minutes. She rolled it in the grass and tickled it with ferns and twirled a twig which it followed with wide glassy eyes then it grimaced and discharged and she was glad because she was able to clean it off with grass and leaves and water from the stream.

As soon as she had finished cleaning it the baby did more and it was runny this time and almost green so she wiped and washed it again. She dressed it wrapped it and re-tied the sling. Then she stood and went back the way she came.

At the edge of the copse the girl stood in the trees a ways and looked out across the fields and at the rolling hills and mountains beyond. They were hazy shapes that appeared to be shifting – those great broad backs of creatures whose heads were hidden in the earth and whose pointed tails snaked away to form unseen valleys. Future destroyers of civilisations.

Soon the fields would give way to those hills and then the hills would become mountains and she knew she would have to go through them and she would have to take the most obscure tracks if they weren't to find her.

She turned and walked to them.

THE GIRL PASSED two old cottages at a distance and entered a young evergreen plantation of firs pines and spruces. She imagined it would one day be a great dark forest that crept south to cover an entire hillside and then in the next century – or the one after that – people would flock there to sunbathe and eat picnics at the dam further up the valley but for now it was a series of ordered saplings no more than twelve or fifteen feet in height and laid out on a grid.

It felt strange to be walking in the young wood. It made the girl feel tall and over-sized and strong and she felt good about this. She pretended she was gigantic; a fearless ogre hounded by the villagers who mistook her lumbering size and eternal silence as a sign of danger. Something to fear. They would flee her presence. No-one could harm her.

Soon she left the wood and crossed a grassy plain and was following a steep track up a hillside. The track climbed at taut diagonals through a series of cutbacks and she bent her back and dug in. She felt exposed on the hillside so the girl walked quickly until the path rounded a corner and then seemed to fade into scrublands. It just ended.

Her heel was sore. It was burning. Every step shot a pain up the back of her leg. She stopped to remove a boot and found there on the ball a large perfectly round blister had formed. It was white and dappled like the surface of the moon.

She manipulated the liquid inside it for a moment and felt something fleshy give beneath her thumb. A creaking of liquid. She did not burst it.

The girl put her boot back on and walked until she passed the edge of more pine trees – older and sturdier this time – then she plucked a needle from one and sat on a log to remove her boot again. The log was a fallen pine now soft and pliable and rotting.

Another memory from before the Sisters took her in; another memory from up top: the sensation of shadows. Less a memory then and more of a feeling. Adult shapes in a cold stone room. Pushing and pulling. Raised voices. Her father striking her mother – she could picture neither of them – then things being tipped and upended in the commotion and her brothers and sisters fleeing – five or seven or nine of them – then the feeling of rapid movement. Of motion. Hands grabbing at her hands – cold and dry – walking on little legs then freewheeling down a hill to the town with women dressed in black and white and a man who looked like something out of a nightmare looking down at her then placing a hand on her head and saying it's alright you're with us now it's alright you're with God now.

Remember not former things. And ancient things consider not.

She kept the baby on her back as she crossed her foot over her other leg and leaned in. She compressed the blister to push the pus into one corner then stuck the needle into the tight bubble. A jet of hot yellow liquid leapt out and droplets splattered her hand. There was more of it than she expected. Then the blister went loose like a deflated balloon; like the reflection of the moon in running water – again the moon – so she dabbed at it with her sock then put it back on and tied her boot tighter and carried on.

4.

THE POACHER SAW that the Priest walked with purpose. His was not the gait of one of these weekend hillside wanderers who had taken to turning up in town in the warmer months nor was it that of natural-born countryman such as a herdsman or farmer or gamekeeper or poacher.

He saw that the Priest worked on town-time and was a watch-wearer and although he was not sensibly pacing himself his energy reserves seemed limitless. The Poacher preferred to let the land do as much of the walking as his legs – it was how he was raised: work with the mountain and not against it. Let the land carry you where it can. Seek shelter when it is needed for it can always be found. Eat when hungry for a meal is always close by. Rest when tired. Do not travel with undue haste for you will fall. You will get there when you get there.

But the Priest seemed to almost take pleasure in making it hard for himself. To the Poacher he seemed intent on taking the shortest rather than the easiest route and in that respect he was like Perses bounding across boulders and slipping clumsily down banks. He was practically panting at the trail. Unbending in his mission.

He had to admit to being impressed with the Priest's stealth and stamina. He seemed unnaturally driven. Fuelled by an inner force. God the Poacher supposed. Christ almighty he thought. The man had barely stopped to take water. Keeping up with him was not a problem of course but the Poacher did wonder at what point the Priest would run out of steam – and then what?

He did not want to be saddled with helping the Priest back down to the town. That he did not want.

The Poacher watched as his companion stumbled over stones and fought against uneven ground occasionally grunting and panting.

You might want to think about slowing up a little bit there Father he said.

And you might want to think about speeding up a little bit there replied the Priest.

I can go as fast as you like but it's you I'm thinking of. You'll wear away your heels away at this rate.

The Priest did not respond.

It's just that I know these valleys well Father.

Again the Priest did not respond so the Poacher repeated himself but this time louder.

I said it's just that I know these valleys well Father. And I know there's only so many routes a dumb lass with half a mind could take. What I mean is we can go as fast as we like but with Persey here we'll flush her out soon enough so we might as well take our own sweet time.

When there was no response the Poacher started whistling one of his favourite drinking songs to fill the awkward gap that widened between them.

I'd prefer to enjoy the silence said the Priest.

The Poacher looked at the back of the Priest's pale thin neck – a neck that unlike his had not seen sun this past season. He looked at the Priest's neck and thought how easy it would be to snap it with some snaring wire and then he idly wondered whether the punishment for putting a man of God in the soil was greater than that of a common man and then he thought of all the different ways he would dispose of a body out here if he had to. Of course pigs were always the best way. Any countryman knew that a half dozen hogs could do to a body in half a day that which time and the elements and the scavengers would take half a year or longer to do. Because it's the bones and the skull that are the tricky parts. And the teeth. Especially the teeth. The hogs can't munch through them. Too small. So the smart man would stick around to collect the hog scat afterwards and then spread it far and wide across the land.

These were the things that occupied the Poacher's mind a lot of the time.

He walked on behind the Priest listening to the muted melody that the breeze played across the fells and the strange harmonies it created around rocks and he heard the screech of a bird – a kestrel by the look of it – high above them. He thought he could hear running water somewhere too and then the insistent bleating of a sheep and then a few moments later the satisfied guttural groan of a cow a long way ahead of them and then a little while after that the screech of two crows first quarrelling and then tumbling together and beneath it all – undercutting it all – the scrape and swish of his oilskin; the panting of the dog and the reedy raspy breathing of the Priest.

There's no silence out here Father he finally said but because it was uttered so quietly and the Priest offered no response the Poacher wondered whether he had even spoken the words out loud at all.

THE GIRL CROSSED the peak of the hill. Her view was obscured by trees and dips in the land but she tried to maintain as straight a line as possible.

The hill formed part of the lower slopes that divided two valleys that ran up to join a vast range of peaks all carved by water. Left untended for hundreds of thousands of years it had run through rock and stone to carve great gorges and glens; to create dales and dells and vales and valleys. Ice and water had made this landscape. First groaning and creaking as the glaciers expanded and shifted then washing and gushing as they melted away to reveal new contours and dominions. A beautiful barren place.

Somewhere along the way she crossed the invisible boundary between Cumberland and Westmorland. One into the other; oblivious and unaware the girl would never know which.

At its peak the hill she found herself on was less than a thousand feet and therefore did not qualify as a mountain. The valley had tracks and paths cutting through it and was scattered with a dozen cottages and smallholdings but the hill was anonymous and unremarkable. Too roughshod and uneven to be habitable. It saw few people and would be written about in no guidebooks.

As she crossed a clearing near the summit of the hill a panic of sound erupted. No more than thirty feet away a disturbed roe deer turned and ran into the trees but there was a fence in its way – an old sagging piece of wire that caught it across its chest and it went sprawling backwards.

The girl stopped and watched. She could see the deer's expanding eyes: wide black fearful and possessed by an instinctive desire for self preservation.

She didn't move. The deer regained its footing and charged at the fence harder this time. It boldly tried to leap the wire but the wire was high and its front legs caught the wire and snagged at the knee as its back legs pushed on forward and for a second it was like two composite parts were doing battle – instinct driving it one way and momentum the other.

The girl stood still so as not to alarm it further. Even the baby was silent as she willed the roe to clear the fence.

She became aware of her own heartbeat and the sound of blood rushing in her ears. Her senses more alive and shifting into overdrive. It was as if she was feeling what the roe felt.

I press on toward the goal for the prize of the upward call of God in Christ Jesus.

The girl watched as the deer bucked and flayed with the scent of the girl and the baby strong in its nostrils. And she too could smell what the roe smelled: the stale funk of sweat and unwashed hot parts. The crust of dust and saliva around her mouth. A clammy festering dampness and stale breath. The lingering hum of urine and faeces and the milky vomit of the baby on her back. Everything was heightened; her smell suddenly musky and sickening.

Everywhere around the girl the undergrowth was creeping and rustling and crackling and seething and breeding and watching. The scrub and thicket was alive and vivid and she was brilliant and she was coursing with adrenalin but still barely daring to draw breath for fear of somehow impinging further upon the territory of the deer.

Then the creature managed to clear the remains of the old wire fence with an energised and ungraceful leap and darted tangentially into the bushes its white rump bouncing arrogantly. Nothing but the quivering of leaves in its wake suggested it had even been there.

The girl felt completely drained of energy. She was suddenly hungry too. Famished. Her head felt light but her limbs felt heavy as she walked across the clearing and out of plain view.

She went into the trees and untied the baby from her back and then flopped down. Though it was difficult to discern she felt she must be resting somewhere on the large flat peak of the covered hill. She turned to look behind her and her breath audibly caught in her throat as she saw through the space between bushes a great lake spread out below her. It was iridescent as it snaked towards a dog-leg bend that ran out of sight around the curved side of a green mountain that loomed so huge it seemed to fill her vision. It was so large that it felt as if she could reach out and touch it. As if it was the entire world or perhaps even bigger.

IT WAS THE pharmacist. The pharmacist kept him supplied. It was he who had first suggested the Priest try this miracle medicine when he returned one day for more syrup for a cough that had been rattling at his lungs like a caged bear for weeks many.

You look tired and run-down Father he said. You should try this. It's new on the market. I take it myself. I have it sent over from Germany. They love it over there.

He handed over a small brown labelled box with the words FORCED MARCH printed on it.

The Priest turned it over in his hand. Inside was a glass vial.

A dose of that when you're feeling a little frayed Father and it'll see you right.

What is it?

They calling it a wonder drug. It's for all-round well being. It gives you pep.

What's pep?

You know. Energy. Vitality.

I don't think I'm interested said the Priest.

I'm no doctor as you know but I'd recommend it Father. I've been taking it myself for lassitude from autumn since and I've never felt better.

What do I do with it?

You can put in your drink or you can rub it on your gums but they say the best way is to inhale some. A little dose up each nostril. Just a nip. It does wonders for the respiratory system. The effect is a little like coffee.

I don't like coffee.

Ah but you see it doesn't taste like coffee. It just gives you a little zip of a morning. Clears up any aches and pains. They're all taking it down in London. It gives you strength and clarity.

Clarity?

Yes. Clarity. Look inside and read for yourself.

The Priest opened it up and withdrew the vial. On the label it said:

Burroughs, Welcome & Co.

'FORCED MARCH'

Containing the combined active principles of

Kola nut and Coca leaves.

~ *Allays hunger and prolongs the power of endurance* ~
'Forced March' will supply the place of food,
make the coward brave, the silent eloquent
and render the sufferer insensitive to pain.

You can have that one for free Father said the pharmacist. A trial if you like. Consider it a gift to the church from we the community. If it helps you it helps us.

The Priest replaced the vial in the box.

Fine. I'll try it. Thank you.

Take it three times a day and that vial should last you a fortnight.

I'll try it.

The Priest turned to leave then paused. And can I expect to see you in church on Sunday?

Of course Father. Of course. Remember: three times a day. And when you run out after a fortnight you just pop back here to see me.

Perhaps I will he said. Perhaps I will.

The Priest was back after six days.

THE BABY WAS crying. The baby was screaming. The baby was hungry.

The girl still had the potato but it was large and hard and raw and she had no way of cooking it so instead she tore strips from the last of the ham then gnawed on it and mixed it with her spittle until her cheeks were packed with the pink pulp. Then she gave the baby spoonfuls of it. As soon as it had gulped the mush down it wanted more. She gave it all the ham that was left and took none for herself but still it cried the unrestrained wail of hunger.

The girl took her dolly rag and loosened the knots that helped form its bodily shape and then smoothed it out then tied it around the baby's ankle. She looped the other end around the base of the bush and then walked inland. She followed the hill and climbed down a small crag that plunged her into a sea of lush green bracken that was growing at shoulder height.

The bracken was in full bloom. Come autumn it would be a brittle and burnt orange turning a flat brown and by winter little more than a graveyard of skeleton branches awaiting fossilisation. But for now it was living whole that carried at its core the summer.

She felt the huge green mountain behind her again. Silently watching. Just knowing that it would be there long after all this was over gave her comfort.

She could hear the baby crying. She walked quickly.

The mountain would watch over it.

A top breeze swept across the surface of the ferns and they swayed. Their fronds followed the weft of the fell's covering. She looked across their surface. She looked at the ripple of movement running at her eye-line then she pushed onwards and out the other side where the bracken abruptly ended and a broad patch of low-growing shrubs began. She bent to examine them. She lifted the leaves and dug into the moss-like base and found what she was looking for: a cluster of small dark bilberries. Their skins were dusted a smoky grey from the dampness and some of them were encased in fine spider's threads. She ate one then another. They were soft and fleshy and sharp as the summer had not yet made them sweet. But they were good enough.

She reached around and picked more. She picked quickly pulling half a dozen off at a time by combing the undergrowth with her fingers then periodically stopping and cocking her head to the breeze to see if she could hear the baby.

The girl mouthed the words: the mountain will watch over it.

She dropped the bilberries into her pocket and searched the patch for more. Her back began to hurt and her forearms and wrists got snagged and scratched and stained with the purple juice of berries. It got under her fingernails and turned them even darker than they already were. She ate as she picked. It took a long time to get a large handful. Her lips became puce.

When she stopped the girl was surprised to see that she had moved fifty feet through the patch and as she straightened she thought she saw the lake before her. But it couldn't be the lake because she had left that behind her and she was facing in a different direction.

A moment of confusion rippled through her. Disorientation and panic. She stopped and turned as she looked around to where she had come from but she could clearly see the virgin path she had cut through the fern and knew that the lake did not extend this far.

The bairn. She couldn't hear it. She couldn't hear the bairn.

The panic turned to relief as she realised she wasn't lost but that there was another body of water through the trees ahead. A different one. A tree-flanked tarn or pond. A mountain-locked elevated body of water.

She put the rest of the bilberries she had collected into her pocket and then turned and ran back through the patch. The wiry springiness of the heather underfoot helped the girl along and then she was running through the ferns and striding up the crag and pulling herself up by handfuls of grass then into the dense thicket where the baby had stopped crying and was now cramming fistfuls of dirt into its mouth.

She grabbed its wrist and put her fingers into its mouth. She brushed away dead pine needles and leaves and arid soil that was glued to its tongue and hard pink gums with saliva.

The girl took some berries from her pocket and pressed them down into the spoon to make a paste then poured it into the babies' mouth. The child winced and its face drew tight but then it relaxed and she fed it more. She picked out stems and stalks from the pulp and purple drool ran down its chin. She repeated the process again and again. The baby stopped crying then coughed up a glob of unchewed berries so she put them back in its mouth and held it shut until it had swallowed.

Then she picked the baby up and held it to her chest and patted its back until it emitted fruity belches.

SHE PUT HER dolly rag and spoon back in her pocket and the baby on her back and began to explore the crag. The ground undulated underfoot. There were many hollows from when the earth had been dented by the tumble of great boulders forced down the conjoining valleys during the melting of the glaciers.

There were fallen trees too. Large rotting trunks tipped sideways to reveal a shock of tangled roots that were mirror images of the dead branches splayed out across the hill. The upended trees and deep roots had torn at the earth to create more holes around their base. One of them was split asunder as if by lightning and some still had rocks and small boulders ensnared in their roots where they now hung suspended six feet above the ground to create a strange primordial wood within a wood. One of mud and root and rock. A world reversed.

Sometimes the girl stopped and stood and looked at the lake as it changed colour. Soon the sun would be going down. She could see boats out there on the water. Tiny white dots. And there were islands. Small tree-filled rocky outcrops rising from the water like the tips of something unknown.

Or perhaps they were floating there; adrift on the surface.

She had heard people say that one of the islands over on Derwentwater floated. They said it was made of marsh weed and only came up to the surface when the gases made it so. The rest of the time it was hidden like a Leviathan of the deep. But sometimes – every few years – it appeared.

They said that if you had the puff and the inclination you could swim right beneath it and come out smiling on the other side. Said there was nothing to keep it tethered.

The girl wished she was on one of the islands now.

The girl wished she and the baby could go there and never see anyone and never leave. She'd teach the bairn to catch fish and climb trees and that would be that. There would be no more running and no more hiding. The child wouldn't need to speak because there would be nothing to say. Language would be unnecessary and they would not need to keep their eyes open during the dark hours; there would be no long cold bodies sliding sideways into their beds. No flesh pinched and twisted. No one to call them dummy.

And on sunny days they would stretch out on the rocks and let the water lap at their feet and in the winter months they would hibernate in a den so well made not a single drop of water would get through its walls and they would be safe and warm like birds in a nest. They would grow vegetables. An old badger would keep the slugs and snails at bay. Bees would give them honey.

She kept on walking. She pushed through layers of thicket so tangled overhead that the light barely reached them and stumbled out the other side into a natural clearing where more trees had once fallen or the ground was too rocky for the roots of parasites to take.

She used a stick to part the thorny vines and barbed creepers before her. She followed animal runs.

There was a tree whose trunk was wide in girth and dry beneath and which must have fallen during the storms of last winter because the leaves were still on it and its branches made a natural shelter from trunk to ground.

If she climbed onto the trunk she could see the lake and the mountain and if she turned she could look up the valley where the flanks rushed to a foreboding incline and formed to scratch a jagged ridge across the sky as if it had been ripped and torn from peak to peak.

She put the baby down and got in there under the trunk and she swept the dirt and leaves to one side then lay on her back and looked up at the pin-prick holes that the weevils had made in the rotting wood.

Then she rolled out and picked the baby up and walked back through the tangled thicket. It was easy to find her way because she had made her own trail and soon she was in the bracken patch on the fell-side.

The baby tugged at her earlobe again the whole way then it fell asleep.

She began to pull bracken stems from the earth at their base. She pulled and tugged but they were more deeply embedded that she expected so she tore and snapped them instead and twice they gouged her arms and twice she stopped to rub the red streaks opening up on her skin.

The girl gathered armfuls of the fronds and stacked them in a pile and then she picked more. When the pile was big she bent and lifted it and it was heavy. With the baby on her back she felt her spine compressing. Her knees and thighs took the strain then she walked unsteadily back up the short steep hill and into the thicket and around the crown of the hill.

She found the tree and crouched to spread the ferns down there. Then she walked back to the bracken patch and picked more and brought them back.

The girl stood to look at the lake again which had become less silver. Now it was dark and still and she looked at the way the mountain's fells plunged straight down into the water over at the far side without even stopping to create a shore.

In places the scree dropped near-vertically into the dark waters and it scared her to think how deep it might be and what lay at the ice-cold bottom of the lake down there and how long it had been this way. The vast unknown of the water made her feel as uneasy as the solidity of the silent mountain provided comfort.

She was sweating again. Her shirt was stuck to her back again. She stopped to rub her scratches again.

The day had been the length of a month.

She slowly walked back to the small crag. Down through the bracken. Across the bilberry patch.

The secreted tarn was through the trees.

It was maybe a hundred or more feet in length and forty feet at its widest part but it was squeezed in the middle to create a figure of eight shape. The tarn was so narrow in the middle you could nearly walk across it. It wasn't deep. It was surrounded by man-planted pines neatly arranged in lines two or three decades earlier.

Flies and skaters broke the surface and the occasional gulping fish rose to feed on them. They were small fish. About a hand's length. Sleek and silvery. Perch probably. The quarry of the pike. Tench perhaps.

She walked around the tarn and into the trees and then sat down.

It was getting dark. The trees across the tarn were becoming washed out through the twilight haze and were blurring at the edges.

She watched the water and listened to the sounds of the birds getting ready to roost. She sat for a long time. She watched the sky turn and the clouds soften and the light wane then she stood and stripped to her underwear and unclothed the baby and walked into the open. She waded into the water.

The cold felt like nails being driven into the soles of her feet. The girl tried to walk quickly but her feet sank into the tarn bed's silt. It billowed up around her as she disturbed it. Turned it cloudy. It felt unctuous on her skin. Oily almost.

When the water came up to her waist and her breath was short she clasped the baby tighter to her bare breast and then turned and pushed herself backwards into the water. It stole the last breath from her lungs – pressed it out of her – and for a few seconds it felt like she couldn't see properly. The baby squealed as the girl's feet scrabbled for the bottom and she lurched and stumbled out of the water. It was too cold. She felt it in her bones. She was aware of her entire skeleton. She dashed back into the trees and took some large breaths.

In the gloaming she studied her naked body and it looked alien to her. Her breasts hung down pale and swollen. The nipples dark. A map of blue veins pulsing beneath the translucent skin. She scraped away a tiny crust of dried milk from her teats.

Her hip bone protruded in a way that seemed odd and detached. She ran her hands down and felt that her calves were covered in hard stubs of dark hair that spread to a finer down on her thighs. It laddered up from her crotch too.

She had not seen herself this way for a long time. And though she had barely eaten there seemed to be more of her than she remembered.

Shivering she felt her way around her body with numb fingers.

As she did something changed. Her skin began to tingle. It became pink and she started to feel warm. Her network of bones no longer ached. The warmth spread from within. The shock of the cold mountain water had awakened her. The shock had enlivened her.

The water was biting as she waded back into it but when she held the baby above her head and submerged herself when she let the water close in over her head it was as if the girl was in a tepid bath. Her body was taking care of itself. Blood and a pulse were all she needed.

She stood and splashed water on the baby and cleaned its parts and cupped some water into its mouth then climbed out and dried it. She wrapped it again and tied it by an ankle to a tree stump again.

The evening had been the length of a year.

Their survival would depend upon these repetitions.

When she turned back to the tarn it was near dark and the moon was dancing on the water that was still rippling from her disturbance. The girl slipped back into it one more time. The girl cleaned herself; the girl washed herself. She floated on her back and pointed her toes to the benevolent face that looked down at her from the sky then she ducked underwater and opened her eyes and stared into the darkness and held herself there her heart beating her blood coursing and feeling utterly hidden; submerged in the night – a part of the stone and the water and the fell and the stars.

5.

SPRING HAD UNFOLDED itself into summer and Mrs Hinckley had coughed the cough of the doomed and the doctor visited her regularly and her husband sulked and seethed with the same look of quiet resentment towards every living thing that the girl had seen in every man and the baby began to grow into its oversized head. This was the girl's new life now. Subjugation again.

She felt a bond with this tiny helpless creature that cried and screamed and excreted though in those moments of quiet when it grabbed onto her finger and stared into her eyes and smiled she experienced feelings that were new and scary and alien and beautiful. Things that neither of the child's parents had ever felt. The feelings grew as the green season spread through the town and up the fells.

The girl began to set aside little things. Items for herself. Food and clothing for the bairn. Things they wouldn't miss. Bits of string. Pens. A bobbin. A knife. Shoelaces. An old newspaper she couldn't hope to read.

The girl had never had possessions before. Ownership of objects was new. So was the love for another entity. A living thing.

She knew that He said *sell your possessions and give to those in need for this will store up treasure for you in heaven* but she had never had the opportunity. In these objects she created secrets and these secrets signalled baby steps towards a daring new direction awaiting exploration.

And the girl began to have original thoughts too. Ideas that developed unfettered and without the Sisters stepping in to call her sinful. Thoughts that went undetected and unpunished.

Thoughts about movement. Thoughts about a new life somewhere in the land beyond. She and the baby together as mother and child. Just the trees and the fells and sky above. Or the island. Somewhere with no-one to bother them. No chores or soot or the fists of drunken men. No interference no violation. No nocturnal visitations. Just she and the baby at peace.

In the moments when she wasn't working the girl began to think about life – about living and feeling alive – perhaps for the first time.

Then the child took ill. For three days its breathing was tight and it became restless. Its sleep pattern broken. The girl tended to it. She warmed milk for it and she cradled it. She sniffed its soft head and she rocked it back to sleep. But the rhythm of the house was disturbed for the duration of the child's illness and Hinckley stomped around the house and complained of plain food and a lack of sleep and anything else he could think of. And the louder he got the more the house appeared to shrink in size.

On the fourth evening the girl was out in the yard tending to the wood pile when she heard the baby wailing. Not crying but wailing. A howl of sorrow; a scream of sickness.

It was a warm clear cloudless evening. She put down the sledgehammer and splitting chock and went into the house. She climbed the stairs and crossed the landing and there he was. In the nursery – in their room. The child's father. Hinckley. Holding the baby aloft. Lifting the baby and shaking the baby. Shouting at the baby. Shaking and shouting shut up shut up for Christ's sake shut up until its scream became locked in its throat and its face began to twist with discomfort. A tragic-looking shadow crossed its eyes.

The baby's face was a dark red as if it were drowning in its own blood; its hands hung loose and head rolled unsupported. She ran into the room and reached for it and her sudden appearance surprised the child's father enough for him to release his hold on its tiny torso and for the girl to take the child to her chest. She turned away from him.

She took out a breast. The sound of breathing filled the room. His and hers.

The child's.

IT'LL BE DARK soon said the Poacher. We should set in for the night.

Set in?

Aye. Make camp.

We're not stopping.

What do you mean?

I mean we're not stopping said the Priest. We'll walk through the night.

And how do you propose we do that Father.

With our feet and God's guidance.

The two men walked in file. The Priest first then the Poacher. The dog circled them running three miles for their one.

It'll be dark.

I thought you were a Poacher.

I am.

Well then. The moon will be out.

We need rest.

He that keepeth Israel shall neither slumber nor sleep.

What's that Father?

Your hangover is your problem. And the way you drag that foot like that. If I had known –

Known what Father?

It doesn't matter.

We'll walk through the night till we find this girl.

What about food?

What about it?

I'm hungry.

You're always thinking about your appetite said the Priest. The hill behind him framed his long head.

You want more than you need he continued. Hunger is a weakness.

But then we're all weak at some point.

Hunger is greed said the Priest. Greed is sinful.

With respect Father everyone has to eat. Aren't you hungry?

You're all consumed by appetite and desire. Do you know why?

Why?

Because you're spiritually empty.

My stomach is empty.

So eat.

I need to catch me something first.

Like what?

Rabbit'd be good said the Poacher.

So catch a rabbit. Then catch me up.

You won't wait for me?

No.

But I'll need to skin it. Clean it. Build a fire. Then cook it.

So do it.

What about the dog Father?

He stays with me. Only the dog can find the girl. We'll go on ahead.

But how will I know how to find you.

You're the poacher.

I know but.

A child's life is as stake and you're thinking about yourself said the Priest. If you want to go hunting rabbits like a didicoy that's your business. But I'm here for a purpose.

Well can we at least rest for ten minutes?

The Priest stopped. He was a dozen paces ahead of the Poacher and as he turned in the crepuscular light he looked paler and more drawn than before. His eyes seemed black. His cheekbones drew triangular shadows on his face and his teeth seemed even smaller. The milk teeth of a man-child thought the Poacher.

Five minutes he said.

I know you won't deny me the call of nature.

Just do what you have to do. Go over there. Behind that crag. I'll go this way.

Aren't you even going to sit? asked the Poacher.

I'll sit if I want to. You just think about yourself.

Fine.

I'll enjoy a break from your rabbiting.

That's a joke isn't it Father. You're having a laugh with me.

He who sits in the heavens laughs said The Priest. The Lord holds them in derision.

The Priest waited until the Poacher had walked uphill and then he walked in the opposite direction and around a house-sized crag. From beneath his collar he lifted a chain over his head and unscrewed a small vial from it. Using the screw as a small spoon he lifted a small heap of powder to his nose and inhaled twice in each nostril. It was hard to see it in the fading light but he felt it clear and precise and searing. The moon was out. A perfect circle. A metallurgical wonder. A steel plate forever welded to the sky.

He looped the chain over his head and breathed deeply.

THE DAYS HAD become longer and clearer and Mrs Hinckley's phlegm thinned and her cough became less violent. She began to spend more time downstairs drinking tea and looking out of the window. Her face a colourless sheet of fell slate.

Here she could watch the birds peck at the crumbs and strips of fat that she left on the bird table.

She saw bullfinches she saw meadow pipits she saw willow tits. Once a redstart.

And she watched the girl when her back was turned. She observed her strangely restricted movements and the tight way she carried herself. Huddled as if to amplify her insignificance or minimise the space she occupied in the world. A shuffling huddle made old before her time.

She was a strange one. Many of the St. Mary's lot were. Damaged goods they were. Bad girls. Born into nothing and then abandoned into even less. Some of them were the bastard children of passing labourers. Some orphaned. Others just born straight backwards.

But the Sisters did God's work. Mrs Hinckley knew that. They were saintly; thankless saviours of these young women.

And this one – she was a worker. No doubt about it; dumb but not stupid. Mute but capable. Good with the child too. She doted on it as if it were her own. Odd but no shirker. Touched by His hand and made simple.

Soon Mrs Hinckley began to do a few light chores to get her strength up. The washing and folding of clothes. Cleaning the pots. The pantry shelves.

That's when she noticed the child's clothes. There were fewer than before. The blue bonnet and some blankets were missing. Two pairs of booties. She checked the dirty clothing basket and the dresser and she checked the line then thought nothing more of it.

Then the spare bib went. And the nappies were down too. She asked the girl about it.

The bairn's missing some clothes she said. Have you seen them?

The girl turned and looked away which wasn't unusual.

Mrs Hinckley laid a hand on her shoulder.

The clothes. Have you seen them.

The girl shook her head.

She left the room.

Walked upstairs.

That night after the girl had been sent on upstairs she raised it with her husband.

The lass. I think she's stealing.

Money you mean?

No. Clothes from the bairn.

How do you work that one out?

There's bits gone missing. Bibs and the like. Blankets.

They'll be in the wash or summat.

I've checked.

Are you sure you've not mislaid them.

I'm sure.

Have you spoken with her?

I raised it.

And how did she respond?

How do you think? Same as usual: with silence.

She'll have to go then he said. Tomorrow.

You think.

First thing sniffed Hinckley. I told that nun there on our doorstep. I told her I'd not tolerate thieving.

Maybe we should give her a day or two. Give her the benefit.

I thought you said you were sure.

I think I am.

Think's not good enough. Would you swear to it?

Mrs Hinckley hesitated.

No.

Well then.

Well then she said. I'll keep a close eye on her.

You do that.

Let the thief no longer steal she said. But rather let him labour – doing honest work with his own hands.

You sound like one of them bloody Sisters you do said her husband.

THE NEXT MORNING the fires weren't lit and there was no tea mashed in the pot. Ash sat in the blackened hearth like dirty snow. Hinckley would have to break kindling and boil his own water for a wash.

And he wasn't about to do that.

He took the stairs two at a time and went into the nursery. It was empty. He crossed the landing into the bedroom. His wife was in bed again. His wife was turned away to the wall again. The curtains drawn again. He put a hand on her shoulder. It was done without tenderness.

Where's the bairn? he said.

She stirred slightly. Groaned.

He shook her harder. Prodded her.

The bairn.

She rolled over and coughed.

In the cot.

The cot's empty.

It can't be.

I've just been in and the bairn isn't there.

I don't –

The bairn isn't there. Where's the girl at?

She went to speak but another cough came out instead. Something loosened inside her. She sat up. Coughed again.

That imbecile he said. Where's she at?

Hinckley back-handed his wife across her papery cheek. Her ears rang and fire spread across her face. It was the first time he had struck since her illness. Since the child.

Listen to me. Where is she? Where's the imbecile?

Hinckley's wife struggled to catch her breath. It caught in her throat before she could speak. She brought her hand to her cheek and looked at her husband.

I thought she was in the room with the bairn.

She's not in the room with the bairn.

She has to be.

Then you're telling me I'm blind woman.

He turned and left the room. He went down the stairs. He bellowed.

Where's my child?

His wife rose from the bed as Hinckley came up the stairs two at a time again and went back into the nursery. He came out. He filled the landing for the moment. A shape cast against the stairwell window.

How long? he said. How long since you saw her?

She was just here. I was sure I heard her.

How long since you *saw* her for Christ's sake.

She searched the landing with her eyes for an unseen answer. Last night she said quietly. After supper. Same as you.

Go to Mary's Hinckley said.

I don't understand.

Go to St. Mary's. She's gone and taken my child with her.

My child stung her. The bairn was their child. More hers than his even. He might have seeded her but it was she who had borne it and she who had birthed it.

Her legs went weak and she grabbed for the banister. She bent double and sobbed. The sob turned into another hacking cough.

She gripped the spherical end of the hand-rail and then rested her forehead on her hand. Saliva hung from her mouth. She spoke through it. Pleaded through it. Created tiny sobbing bubbles with it.

Why has she gone?

God only knows. She could be hours away. Now go to Mary's.

I don't feel well.

Go to Mary's and fetch the Priest.

She looked up at Hinckley. She wiped away the saliva.

The Priest?

He nodded. She sobbed again.

Hinckley pushed past his wife and barrelled down the stairs. He reached for his coat.

We can find her ourselves she said.

He snorted.

And what use are you?

Please she said. Why the Priest – why *him*?

He'll know what to do. She's one of his. He knows them girls inside and out.

Do you think –

Hinckley cut her off.

I'll fetch him up myself.

A cold draught blew in from the street then he was gone. The door swinging on un-oiled hinges behind him.

A MEMORY THAT she had often re-visited in the darkest days of St Mary's – one of the few she had left: the sound of rain on the wood-store roof in which she had hidden and the ice cold mornings when they made her sleep there in that first place that was her home. She recalled being on the moors in snow – up top and alone. At play her brothers and sisters must have fled and left her. Snow obscured her view. It surrounded her and made her think the world had ended and everyone had died and only she was left. She remembered how good this made her feel. Her fingers toes hands cheeks and nose were numb when she was found what seemed like hours but may have only been minutes later. Disorientated and starving but silent. The tears that came were not at being lost but at being found.

AND NOW NEITHER the outdoors nor the night and its infinite darkness held any fear for her. The night was not a foe. In the wood beneath the trees the girl could not see her hand in front of her face or her feet on the ground but the darkness itself was not something to fear.

The girl was not afraid of ghosts or spectres; neither apparitions nor jack o' lanterns black dogs boggles wraiths or the green men that were said to stalk the woods and hollows and fells of the north country. Those that the other girls had told tales of. No. It was people that made her fearful. People and their ways. No animal nor fireside fairy tale creation could harm her here beneath the tree with the bairn in her armpit. But a person could. Especially a person out creeping on the hillside under the concealment of night.

The dark did not scare her but those it could hide did.

The Lord is with me; I will not be afraid. What can man do to me?

The girl had made a nest for herself from the bracken. A primitive grounded eyrie.

She buried herself down in it then pulled the bigger fronds over herself. There was moss for a pillow as night flooded around her.

Her eyes slowly closed then darted open then she closed them and soon she couldn't tell the difference. And soon she was sleeping.

She was damp and stiff when she awoke. All around her dew had gathered on the bracken and ferns and freshly-spun cobwebs like ship's rigging hung heavy with tiny silver droplets vibrating as the spiders crawled across them to gather their night's bounty. For a few moments everything was silent.

A bird started singing and then another and then the conversation grew all around her.

The girl was dry in her nest. She was dry and she did not want to move.

She wanted to stay there forever half-buried in the dirt.

She lay with the baby pulled tight to her chest. It had cried a lot in the night. Howls of hunger. She had had to open her coat and lift her shirt for it in the darkness of night as all around her the grass and leaves rustled. But she had been barren and nothing had come and she didn't understand why and it kept on crying so much that it had exhausted itself and was now sleeping. She was about to lift her shirt again to see if she could squeeze something out – just a few watery droplets from her teat – when something made her blood run cold.

There not more than ten feet away in front of her up against a small log were four tin cans. A band of artificial colours and blocked-out lines unfamiliar against the jumbled green tones of the scrub.

She scanned the clearing looking for other disturbances. Her eyes flitted from left to right and then back again then the girl waited for a few minutes before squeezing herself out from beneath the trunk. She leaned against it a few moments and scanned the thicket again. Watching for movements. Listening for sounds. Then when all she could hear were the birds singing their morning chorus and the rumble and gurgle of her own stomach. She stood and walked the few paces to the tins.

They had been carefully placed and neatly ordered with their labels facing outwards. The first one had a label that was red on the top half and green on the lower and had words written on it.

But all she saw were colours and the black blocks and curves of the lettering.

She picked each up and turned them in her hand. Lying on the ground in front of them was a tin opener and a small tinder box on a lanyard. She opened the box and there were matches in there and laid on top of the matches a small piece of charcloth. She closed the tin.

She looked around again then pocketed the box and walked around the back of the trunk and while supporting the baby inside her coat with one arm she squatted and lifted her skirt and urinated. When she had finished the girl went back to the tins and laid the baby down. It was damp with its own urine. She placed the tins in a fold at the bottom of the sheet that she had used to cover herself in the night then put the baby above them then re-tied it and turned to start quickly walking away.

It was early. The day was a fresh candle just lit and her feet got wet and the lake sat behind a haze. She left it behind as she pushed through whin and thicket and rounded the circumference of the top of the hill.

She tried to not to think about the tins and where they had come from.

Every time the girl thought of the tins she felt scared and she quickened her pace. Once or twice she considered untying the sheet and taking the tins and throwing them as far as she could through the trees and down the hill to disturb the stillness of lake though it was too far away to reach – and her hunger too great to do anything so futile.

The thicket opened out onto a crag that she was able to walk down and around and into more gorse through which there wound a series of paths. The birds were singing more loudly than ever and above her the sky was clear and cloudless.

When she felt like enough distance was between her and the log under which she had slept the girl sat down. She untied the baby and spread out the sheet and unwound it from its blankets and laid them out to dry in the sun. She played with the bairn a while then she reached for one of the tin cans. She looked at the label and then took the tin opener and began to open it. She fumbled and dropped the opener twice but managed to pierce the lid and then took another sniff. The smell was sharp the smell was red the smell was delicious and she took a long drink from the can.

The girl sat the baby up and poured some watery liquid on the spoon and fed it to the baby who swallowed it all straight down then urged her to pour more by grasping the handle of the spoon. She tipped more liquid from the can and fed the baby then did it again. She was about to discard the can but it still had weight so she shook it and heard something move inside of it. A weighted thud. She took the can opener and began to work it along the rim of the can some more. When she had cut halfway around she was able to jam the opener into the gap and bend the lid back.

She looked inside and saw some bright red shapes like huge blood clots. She lifted one out and sniffed it then ate it. A tomato. Skinned and smooth. It was gone in two chews. She had another then another. The fourth she chewed then regurgitated for the baby who pulled a face but still ate half and then spilled the rest down its front. She chewed more for it then gave it the last of the watery red juice.

Then there was a voice:

I wandered lonely as a cloud.

The girl jumped and the can slipped from her grip. There was a man standing close by at the edge of the thicket. He was not looking at her. She recoiled. She reached for the baby and scrabbled backwards with her feet but he just stood there scratching the whiskers on his chin and squinting at the sky and talking as if to himself.

That floats on high o'er vales and hills. When all at once I saw a crowd – a host – of golden....baby toms.

He turned to her.

They always say breakfast is the most important meal of the day. My humblest apologies if I startled you.

The girl looked around for a rock to throw at him but the man didn't seem to notice or was unafraid of how she might react.

Instead he slowly stepped out of the thicket and stood before her.

Nice spot for it he said. Breakfast I mean. Lovely day too. Been here for many an *al fresco* lunch myself.

He was the oddest looking man she had ever seen. His face was lined and crumpled inwards as if to protect his features from the elements and he was extremely thin and wearing a wide-brimmed hat and a tan jacket with many pockets sewn on at strange angles with long clumsy stitches. He also wore an open-necked shirt and trousers that had been rolled back high above his knees to reveal white pipecleaner legs. A coiled rope was slung across one shoulder and a piece of rag was tied around his neck. He carried a backpack.

He was unshaven and a cigarette dangled from his mouth as he talked. His age was indistinguishable. He could have been forty or he could have been double that.

The girl could smell him too. A heady mix of tobacco and sweat and moss and something sweet but repellent like rotting fruit.

Yet when he spoke it was in a voice at odds with his appearance. His vowels were crisp and warm and from elsewhere. From the lowlands.

Please allow me he said. Mr Tom Solomon – short for Thomas not tomato: professor of the woods; doctor of the earthy elements; erudite troglodyte; self-taught tailor; ornithologist; observer of the seasons, culinary wizard; Lakeland tour guide; death-defying conqueror of cliffs crags ridges rocks escarpments arêtes peaks precipices parapets bluffs chimneys and all manner of other dangerous yet wondrous geological developments. At your service.

As he said this he lifted his hat and gently bowed his head then theatrically replaced it.

He spoke in a way that the girl had never heard before. Compared to the flat cloddish delivery of Westmorland folk it sounded more like a melodic song from a place a long way away.

Beware false prophets. They come to you in sheep's clothing, but inwardly they are ferocious wolves.

I thought you could use some supplies he said.

The girl looked at him.

He pointed to the empty tin.

The girl looked at the tin then back to the man.

Consider it camper's etiquette he continued. I saw you were out bivvying but didn't notice much in the way of munch so I thought I'd offer up this lot.

The man awaited a response but when one didn't come he carried on talking.

One should never underestimate the importance of food he said. Personally I favour the vegetarian diet. Neither hoof nor snout nor anything else bestial besides has passed these lips in many a year. Could be a decade. Could be two. I forget now but I still dream of the day when people's tastes will turn and they might start respecting their fellow creatures. Trust me: the future will be defined by our culinary intake. They can invent as many new labour-saving machines as they like but they'll be no good to anyone if we're all bunged up. Constipation can kill.

He prodded the ground with his stick again.

But until that meat-free future comes I suppose some of us will just have to lead by example. There's spare pears too. I've no call for them. I mean I *like* them – don't get me wrong – but they don't like me. Give me the gas they do. Right bad. One nibble and I'm quacking like an angry mallard all night long. Reckon the creatures of the wood think there's a beast in the old Cave Hotel instead of old Tom Solomon.

The man smiled. Sighed.

You can't win them all. Anyway. Don't let me stop you and the little one partaking in your early morning regalements. Beans are good breakfast food. And what's good enough for the homesteading cowboys of the American dustbowl frontier is good enough for us folk I reckon. There's a tin of them too.

The girl held the baby close to her chest and blinked at the man again. He carried on talking.

I've not eaten yet today myself. Thought I'd have an early climb first. Get the blood pumping you know. It pays to burn a little energy before replacing it. Get a sweat on. Lovely day for it too. You and the bairn having a little break from it all I'd wager. Can't blame you. Does you good to get beyond those stone walls and off the cobbles and creaking floorboards. All those straight lines and right angles. Dust everywhere. It's no good is town life. Feels good to go feral from time to time though. Of course it does. Because you can't feel lonely with nature as your companion. Days I can go without seeing a single soul or uttering a single word and I bloody love it – excuse my French dear Napoleon. More folk should try it – *but no*. They'd rather stop indoors where the view stays the same.

The man made a noise with his mouth – *tsk* – shook his head then continued.

Me – I would rather sit on a pumpkin and have it all to myself than be crowded on a velvet cushion. An American chap called Thoreau wrote that. And I can't blame you for holding your tongue either young lady. The Cistercian monks make a career of it. Vow of silence they call it. Part of me can see the appeal but then I like a bit of singalong as well as a natter so I can't imagine the two are mutually compatible. Anyroad. You've no doubt heard me huffing and bellowing like the Lakeland steamer down there or if you haven't I imagine you've heard of me around town. The silly old goat that lives in the cave on the crag. I wouldn't believe all that you hear dear unless it's about my sumptuous cooking and silver tongued way with the local ladies or the time I scaled the Matterhorn with naught but a ham sandwich and forty filterless Gauloises for company. In which case – please – believe away. Because Tom Solomon has never been one to let the truth get in the way of a good yarn and that's no lie. Coffee?

The girl was so overcome by the man's deluge of words and strange speaking voice that she had barely noticed that he had dropped to his haunches and removed his backpack and was now unpacking an oddly-shaped coffee pot and a small bundle of kindling. He unwrapped a twist of paper that contained coffee grounds which he poured into the top part of the pot.

It was too late for her to turn and run.

Water's already in there he winked. Pays to come prepared.

He struck a match and lit the kindling and then sat back on his haunches and felt around his top pocket.

Gasper?

He offered the girl the cigarette packet. She shook her head.

Take one for later?

She shook her head.

For the child then? I'm only pulling your leg. Maybe just as well. They say it's habit forming – mind you they do keep you as regular as a Swissman's ticker.

WHEN THE COFFEE was made the man poured it into two cups then passed one to the girl.

He lit his cigarette and brushed a shred of tobacco from his lower lip and then took a big pull. He exhaled through his nose and the girl thought of a bull in a field on a cold winter's morning.

There's no milk I'm afraid he said. I forgot to pack the cow this morning. Anyway they say too much dairy is bad for your movements. A doctor told me that. Fella by the name of Wilfred Wimpole. Can you believe that? Wilfred Wimpole. Knew him in my London days. A long time ago now. An alcoholic. Gin was his thing. Let me ask you something: would you trust a man with that name? It hardly matters now anyroad. Expect he's dead. Best finish them tomatoes before the Lakeland ants have them.

He gestured to the can with his stick.

The girl looked at it tipped to one side then picked it up. She peered into the tin then she tentatively offered it to the man.

Best not he said. I'll be quacking all the way up the crag. On second thoughts a touch of go-fast gas could be a real boon to an old fella like me.

He winked at the girl then sipped at his coffee.

Only joshing you.

The girl sniffed at her coffee then took a sip. It was foul and black. She winced.

Seeing her reaction Tom Solomon said it's not a proper cup unless you can stand your spoon up in it said the man. Least that's my opinion. I tend to forget not everyone likes it as tough in the mouth as me mind. Developed a taste for it during a trip

86

to Italy. The Alps. You ever been? Wonderful place. Wonderful. God's country if you happen to believe in him – which as a good socialist and devout atheist I don't though on a clear day up the Weisshorn or the Gran Paradiso even an old cynic like me would be inclined to think otherwise.

He drained his cup and flicked the sediment into the fire. It was already burning down to its embers. He smacked his lips.

Yes. God's country.

He pulled on the last of the cigarette then added it to the remains of the fire.

How old's the little one?

The girl held the baby tight to her chest and the man looked away. He didn't appear offended. Instead his face was blank for a moment as he stared into the dwindling flames then he raised his eyebrows and his face brightened.

Here – have you heard about this Cumbrian sheep-counting? A shepherd over in Grange taught us.

The girl looked at him then shook her head.

The man smiled. No? Oh you'll like this. It's a good one. Pure poetry.

Then he started counting out the words with his fingers.

Yan tan tethera.

He stuck out his thumb then his forefinger and index.

That means one two three. Methera pimp and sethera is four five and six. Now let me see.

He looked at his second hand.

Then there's lethera hovera dovera. Seven eight nine. And then dick is ten.

The girl stared at him.

So it goes yan tan tethera methera pimp. Sethera lethera hovera dovera dick. Doesn't that sound so much better than the language we use to express our numerals? And I know what you're thinking young lassie: where the hell do you go from here? Well I'll tell you: yan-a-dick tan-a-dick tethera-dick is where you go from here.

Eleven twelve thirteen he continued. Methera-dick is fourteen. And then we're at bumfit. Bumfit. Fifteen. I love that. And then the rest rolls right off your tongue: yan-a-bumfit tyan-a-bumfit tethera bumfit methera bumfit giggot. Giggot is twenty and that's as high as it goes. You don't need to go any higher. Why would you? All you need to do is go back to one and remember you've still got that first twenty counted off left over and banked up here.

He tapped his temple with a bony finger.

Keep it simple I say. Why bother crowding your head with numbers you'll never need just for counting sheep. It makes perfect sense when you think it over. Only use what you need. There's a lesson to be learnt there.

Only use what you need he said again more quietly this time.

Tom Solomon picked up a pebble from the ground and tossed it in the air and caught it then rolled it in his palm. Even though the girl didn't like the taste she sipped at her coffee again. It was the first warm thing to pass her lips in days.

All that shepherd talk – it's nearly as old as this stone he continued. Or as old as the stone walls they made with them anyway. Folk have been farming these fells as damn near long as they've been living on them. That's how they survived. And they had to find a way to count the sheep in and out the folds. You'll still hear it now on the tongues of some of the fellas. Not many but it lives on. And now you know it too. I've passed it on to you. Now you can count like a Cumberland shepherd and all. And a Westmorland one too come to think of it.

The man stood and as he did his knees cracked.

Find it pays to learn something new every day if you can he said. Even when you're old like me.

He looked into his empty coffee cup.

You know what else I like about these parts? he said while jiggling the pebble in his palm. One of many things anyway. The names of the places. All the name of the little hamlets and fells and dales and crags – they're like poetry to me. Years I spent rotting away in an office down in London and I think I can say with some degree of authority that they've got nothing on our place names up here. Nothing. Down there I reckon they decided on street names and the like by committee. Whereas up here names just emerge over time. They've got Burnt Oak and Knightsbridge down there – granted – but up here there's a plethora of evocative names. So now whenever I hear one that I like I write it down. I collect them you see. Some people like to read literature – me I read maps and make lists. Do you want to hear some?

The man reached into his top breast pocket and removed a small notepad. He licked his thumb and then slowly turned the pages.

Oh – here we go. Expect you've heard most of them mind. There's Snarker Pike. Troutbeck Park. The Hundreds. The Knight. Catstycam – everyone knows that one. Then you've got The Tongue and The Great Tongue. There's Seat Sandal and Seldom Seen. There's Dollywaggon Pike over that way.

The man jerked his thumb over his shoulder.

I might have a wander up there tomorrow. Lovely views. What else have we got? Oh yes. Lyulph's Tower. Ponsonby Fell. Prison Crag. That's a good one. Doesn't sound very inviting does it. That's not far from here either – only a day's walk over past Hartsop way and not far above Hayeswater Gill. Then you've got Loadpot Hill. Crookabeck. Beulah. And Tongue Ho. That's a good one.

The man put his notepad back into his pocket and then poured the grounds from his coffee pot and shook it off into the bushes.

Well he said. I best be making tracks. That cliff isn't going to climb itself.

He looked at the sky.

Reckon there'll be rain this after if not before. Reckon you'd be best to make a move now or bed down in that camp of yours for the day. The sky says it's going to be torrential and I've never known the sky to lie.

He kicked the toe of his boot into the dirt. The girl looked at his bare legs. His shins were shiny and hairless and streaked with dirt. She could smell him again. It was stronger this time now that the fire had nearly stopped smoking and the coffee was gone.

Either way if it rains it'll sure enough stop again. And if you get wet you'll be dry again. And if you're stuck you can always come stop in at old Tom Solomon's cave.

He pointed over in the direction of the valley beyond the tarn.

It's just a gentle couple of miles upstream then when you've passed the old mine you take a steep right up into the wood. From there you'll see two paths. What you need to do is take the top one a ways and – well you'll find it eventually. There's only one cave that I know of and only one Tom Solomon. Just listen out for the singing.

He went to turn then stopped.

He put down his pack and rifled through it. He removed a blanket.

Reckon the little one could use this.

He passed it to the girl.

The girl stood and took it then dug into the bottom of the child's sheet and pulled out the potato. She held it out to the man.

He smiled.

Well that's very kind of you young lady but I've no call for that. My stores are more than full and what I don't have mother nature will provide. You keep it for yourself and the bairn. Mind it's a monster spud that one. It'll bake nicely in the coals.

Then he raised his hat and turned and left.

6.

THE ONLY THING he feared was sleep-talking. If he spoke in his sleep he might reveal his secrets: might let those soul-locked demons of the subconscious out and incriminate himself. That's why The Priest knew he would never lie long in the company of another living person.

The Priest had talked in his sleep since childhood.

And now in adulthood spaces could be shared and appetites sated but sleep beside another was out of the question. There were things that had gone on that no-one needed to know about and intimacy was the key to unlock those secure secrets.

It was society. It was cut through with misunderstanding. He knew his appetites were selective. He knew he enjoyed niche flavours. He was ahead of his time that was all. Hadn't the dignitaries and ruling overlords of the Roman empire exercised and appeased such similar interests two thousand ago? Yes they had. Because it was their right. Their privilege.

And privileges were the church's way of rewarding those chosen to do God's work. Small rewards for a great task: shepherding the sheep into His fold. One day his tastes would be commonplace but until then he would utter no nocturnal revelations if he could help it.

Was it his fault he was superior to these ingrates illiterates and inbreds? No it most certainly was not. To be a physically mentally sexually racially and philosophically advanced human was why he was chosen to do God's work. That was plain to see. And this was all part of the test – to be sent to these harsh northern lands and to not only survive amongst the uncivilised but to *thrive.* To thrive and reign; to control his adopted kingdom in order to spread the word. To tame the flat-tongued heretics.

Yes. To tame the lost wild beasts of his flock. Yes. Everything he did he did for the church. Yes. For Him. Yes. He was making the best of it. Yes. And his faith was as strong as it had ever been. Stronger even.

His interests in the esoteric and the marginal were one of the reasons the seminary had first appealed all those years ago. Because when you are a Priest they elevate you above the commonplace. They lift you up and set you apart and they leave you be. The community respects your silence. They know you're doing God's business and that comes with a certain cachet. It brings insight and insight brings burdens and burdens need an outlet. Being one of His envoys takes its toll.

He had few outlets for these secret compulsions he carried around inside of him but sleep-talking was one of them. Many a night his own words had awoken himself; garbled confessions of things that could never be spoken in daylight. Could never be shared. Heard out loud such descriptions of these desirous impulses had shocked even him and it made them somehow tangible and real and confirmed that they not only existed within the darkest corners of his imagination but had sometimes been acted upon too. And yet still he was not sated. And still wanted more. It was a hunger of sorts.

The Priest vowed never to let himself become so publicly vulnerable. The conscious would take control and the subconscious of the somnambulist world would be kept in the solitude of his bedroom.

So he sat in darkness and he sniffed and felt the air in his lungs. He watched the Poacher crumple and curl in the bracken no better than the beasts of the fells and woodlands that filled his pantry.

He felt his lower jaw circulate and his teeth quietly grinding. And he watched the Poacher's form melt into the night until he was nothing more than a moonlit shape in the dirt and was glad that his travelling companion had finally stopped talking.

THE GIRL DIDN'T feel like walking. She didn't know what to make of the strange thin man in his hand-made clothes and his stories and his funny way of talking either; she didn't know how she felt about him. But for once it wasn't fear.

If he could find her up on the hill under the log in the dead of night then he could surely find her most anywhere. He could hunt her and follow her any time he wanted. He could be hiking into town right now to tell everyone that he had found her to tell them that he had located the imbecile girl with the bairn and hurry hurry because she's up on the lower slopes eating tinned pears. Just look for the wood smoke you can't miss her.

But she doubted that. She didn't know why but for once she just had to take the risk that perhaps not every human wanted to use or destroy her.

So she would rest and she would eat and then she would be strong and she would leave.

The baby was making a smacking suckling sound.

She wondered if that man that smelled bad and gave her the food really lived in a cave like he said and if he did what it was like in there.

If she had a cave she would fix it up nice. She'd make a bed from bracken and there'd be blankets for her and the bairn and she would have a fire burning all the time. She would see that it never went out and she'd hunt and they'd never grow hungry and then when the baby was a bit older and could walk it could hunt too. There would be a waterfall running down that they could wash under and maybe they'd have a chicken or two running loose in the woods and each morning they would go on an egg hunt for breakfast. She would teach the bairn about life by showing it life.

And they would be happy.

After she packed away her things the girl went to the toilet and then smelled that the baby had done the same so she walked back to the tarn's edge. She moved slowly this time. She took small steps and the baby felt heavy and the smell of its scat was strong. It cried all the way.

She walked slowly because every bit of energy would be needed for whatever lay around the corner.

Anxiety ate at her. It's what stopped her being starving all the time.

She worried about dogs and the police and the Sisters at St Mary's and she worried about the Hinckleys and the farmer who had tried to have her in the night and the funny smelly man who said he lived in a cave. She worried about food and sleep and warmth. She worried for the bairn. And she worried about the Father.

You're the lucky one the Sisters had said. Being tapped the way you are. That was the way God wanted and don't you dare to doubt that. Father chose you because you were the quiet one. No other reason but that. He said you'd never be guilty in the language of gossip or hearsay; said the silent can always be trusted because God took their tongues and made them blessed. Said they were gifted in discretion. Receptacles for The Truth. You should consider yourself lucky; your debt to Father is great.

She felt that debt about her now like the ox feels the yoke.

SHE GOT TO the tarn and took off her boots and then her socks and she undressed the baby. She walked out into the shallow nearside end and she bent down and washed the bairn. She scraped the excrement from its scut with her fingers then used dry moss to pat it. She wrapped the baby in the new blanket and then washed its sheet in the tarn.

The water was cold the water was bracing the water set her flesh to tighten. It felt worse somehow being in it up to the knees than fully submerged as she had been the night before. Her feet were sensitive to the water's bite. Again she thought of nails being driven into them; she thought of Jesus on the cross in the chapel in town. She thought of bleeding stigmata. She thought of eternal martyrdom.

She scrubbed the sheet with rocks until the stains were gone then twisted and wrung it. She squeezed every drop she could out of it. She cupped some water into her mouth then sat on a rock and put her socks and boots back on.

She picked more bilberries. She picked for a long time and collected them in the empty pear tin and when it was nearly full she left and walked through the bracken and up the crag and across the clearing and into the scrub and back to her fallen trunk.

The baby was sleeping so she went back to pick more bracken. She stacked as many fronds as she could. It was warm now and she was sweating but the sky was restless and the air felt tight. She could feel it like a steel band around her head. The sky looked like it could snap at any time. For a few minutes everything was still.

The fronds were piled so high in her arms the girl could barely see where she was walking but the route felt familiar now so she carefully picked her way back to the fallen tree where the baby lay. For now she would not flee. The sky had spoken and the sky had said stay.

She took the longest of the bracken branches and wove them into those that protruded from one side of the tree to strengthen the natural canopy that had already formed. It was easy to do and she had soon made a thick green thatch that ran from the backside of the fallen trunk down to the ground. The other side opened out onto the clearing.

She hurried back to the bracken patch and snapped off more. The stalks scratched at her hands and she wished she had a knife then she remembered the lid from the tin of pears so she ran back to get that. She folded it over and then she had a sharp edge with which to cut the stems at the base. She worked quickly and with purpose. The girl stopped once or twice to look at the sky again then she carried the second load back and laid them down in her den.

The baby had its eyes open now.

The girl rolled out from beneath the trunk and walked across the clearing to where there were more rotten branches and she dragged them across to her tree. A breeze was lifting and the sky was tight like the skin of a drum. Somewhere in the far distance she could hear a rumble. Then the valley behind her growled and she stood and saw a breeze ripple across the lake as if a great shoal of fish had risen at once.

Moving quickly now she stripped the old boulders of the thick green moss that covered them and she put that down into her nest too. Then she broke down branches and stacked them under the tree. She gathered more and she stamped them and smashed them and found twigs for kindling then rolled one or two larger logs across the clearing and then found some stones which she also rolled over.

Then she was tired. Then she needed to sit down. The sky growled again – a hungry yawping sound. She crawled beneath the tree and inspected the canopy she had made and there were only a few small gaps where she could see through it. She picked the baby up and petted it for a while then put it down and decided to do an inventory of her possessions. She unwound the damp blanket in which she was storing everything and lined up her items in front of her.

There were the two tins. She also had the potato and the matches and the tin opener; the empty pear tin now contained the freshly-picked bilberries. She also had the bent tin lid and the blanket that the man had given her that the baby was coddled in. It was a lot more than she had yesterday.

The air became charged. It was almost crackling and everything took on a strange sepia hue. Even the birds stopped singing. Only in their absence did she notice them.

The valley boomed.

She pulled the baby tight. It put its arms around her neck and its chin on her shoulder. The girl ran her palm over its smooth head and combed its fine covering of hair with her fingers. She looked at its features: its small flat shiny nose and wet pursed mouth and the long curve of the protruding forehead. It seemed to have changed since the last time she had looked. It was growing. Forming and transforming. Changing shape. Day upon day it was becoming something else right before her.

Overhead the clouds rolled and moiled and they looked like great crashing white waves in a storm though the girl had never seen the sea. Only in pictures. All she knew was land-locked rock and stone and slate and scree; sky and grass and streams and fire. A remote farm. A stone dormitory. Blankets on the floorboards of a loveless house.

The sky. She felt it pressing down.

There was a flash – a violent blink of purple – then a crack of thunder that bounced between the mountains to create an almighty applause.

The rain came again first as slowly elongated drops and then it fell harder and faster.

The baby's eyes widened.

It came straight down driving into the ground with force and violence. The girl thought of the forge in town where the men welded and braced and hammered to drive hot metal into shape through brute force. She thought of the clanging and the banging and the hissing as she had passed it and the narrow eyes of the silent men that stared out at her from the darkness. Streaks of dirt on their taut bare chests and their black faces. White teeth flashing between wet leering lips.

The girl gathered the bracken and pulled the fronds over the two of them then she laid down on her back to let the baby take her teat which had become wet and charged like the sky.

THE PRIEST SPOKE.

Your leg.

Yes.

You limp.

What about it.

How did that occur?

How did I get my limp?

Yes.

I didn't think you cared Father said the Poacher.

I don't.

So why ask.

Because you're slowing us down by at least one mile an hour. One mile an hour over a day – that could be twelve miles we're losing because of it. Because of you. Suppose we begin travelling at the same speed as the girl. By nightfall she'll be twelve miles ahead of us. And that's assuming we're even going in the right direction. So I'm curious.

It was morning and sleep still fogged their eyes. Warm parts chafed under damp clothing as they walked and the Priest carried himself with an even more determined sense of purpose – as if the hills were there to be assaulted and conquered and owned. Availed of all mystery. They were God's obstacles. Nothing more. The Poacher was unhurried in his movements and the panting dog looked at him sideways for instruction.

Curious is it Father said the Poacher.

Yes.

About my limp.

That's what I said didn't I.

My limp.

Why do you have to turn every conversation into a long drawn out charade?

I think it's the first real question you've asked me Father. I'm just surprised.

The girl has taken a child said the Priest. A baby. A living breathing creature created by God. A baby that belongs to someone. To people. To people who are in my parish; who are in my congregation. The girl is my responsibility and the child is my responsibility. Now I know the greatest responsibility you've ever known is to fill your stomach with meat and beer but this matters. If we do not find the girl soon the child may die. The child may already be dead. And then it is on our heads.

It's not on my head shrugged the Poacher.

Yes said the Priest. Yes it is. We will have the community to answer to.

I'm just here to guide you that's all. That's what you said. I'm just here for my knowledge. The bairn's life has nowt to do with me. It's not me what took her.

And if you don't help me find them you might as well have taken that baby and stabbed it through the heart yourself with that pocketknife of yours and fed it to your dog because soon that helpless child will be nothing but useless dead meat if you don't get a move on and do what it is I had paid you to do.

The Priest said this without drawing breath.

The Poacher listened for a moment then he said I'll tell you then Father.

Tell me what?

About my leg.

I'm really not that interested now.

Well I'll tell you anyway and then you can decide if you're interested.

This is what I mean. A long drawn out charade of wasted words. Wasted words equal wasted energy. Wasted energy slows us down. You're making yourself into a murderer of children.

I'm no murderer of children Father and your God can strike me down here and now if that's what he thinks. He's already punished me the once.

If I had known –

Known what Father? said the Poacher.

That I was travelling with a bloody cripple.

That's not very Christian of you Father. What does the Bible say about the sick and the needy?

You don't look sick and needy to me. Just impeded.

That's as maybe Father. But I am injured. Struck down I was. It must have been a quarter century ago now. I was not yet a teenager. It was winter.

Let me guess: you tripped over during Bible study.

Sarcasm Father. It suits you no more than a bonnet and rouge would.

I'm being sarcastic because I know what you are going to say.

How can you know Father? Do you read minds as well as judge us ordinary everyday folk?

I have spent entire months – maybe even years – of my life listening to the confessions of your kind –

My kind?

Yes said the Priest. Uncivilised idiots. Earthy folk. The stricken. You're much the same. My ear has long been trained to your banal stories of self-inflicted woe and hardship. Adultery poverty incest skullduggery. inter-breeding. Your tawdry animalistic existences in your pigsty hovels. I have a good idea what your lot are going to say before you even say it. You're not exactly deep and erudite thinkers around these parts are you.

I thought you cared about your congregation?

All I care about is serving Him snapped the Priest. Everything I do is for Him. If I had it my way I wouldn't have to listen to another mangled word of English from your ugly rotting mouths. If I had it my way I'd whip your stupid eyes. But such is the way of this calling. And as you yourself said you're not a believer so why should I care about you or your gammy leg or any of your other misfortunes. You are a sinner and you are going the way of all sinners: to hell.

If the Poacher was insulted he did not show it.

What about this girl then? he countered. The imbecile. Is she going to hell too for her physical afflictions and humble beginnings?

My point is I know fine well you lost your foot in a man trap while out thieving or contracted gangrene due to neglect or a lack of vitamins or a wall fell on you while you were sodomising your sister or maybe debridement by maggots went awry or your father held your foot in the fire because you spilled his hallowed nightly libation –

You're not from Cumberland are you Father?

No.

Or Westmorland.

No.

Or the countryside of the northlands.

No.

Where then?

It doesn't matter.

I'd like to know said the Poacher. I really would.

Well you'll have a long wait.

Why are you so full of hatred Father?

I wasn't aware I was.

Oh I would definitely say you are.

You don't know anything about me.

I've seen and heard enough.

You've seen and heard nothing.

I've heard plenty smirked the Poacher. You cut quite the figure around town in your cape. A different nun with you every time. People talk.

People are stupid.

Tongues do wag Father.

The words of the wicked lie in wait for blood but the speech of the upright rescues them.

All I'm saying is –

Where is the girl? said the Priest.

What?

Where is the girl? he said again. Do your job and answer the question.

I believe she'll have headed for the lake Father but the lake is busy on these summer days and I reckon the crowds will have put the fear in her. So she'll have carried on and be headed for the next town over Father. She'll go where the food is. You'll not need telling that's some thirty odd hard miles over crag and boulder yet. Likely she'll take a back way though. Away from prying eyes. She'll surface sooner or later – if she makes it. The hills can be cruel if you've got nowt about you. We just need to keep our eyes open. We'll find her and the bairn though dead or alive I couldn't say.

THE RAIN FELL for a long time. It pecked at the soil and flattened the leaves on the trees and drenched the carpet of needles and the clumps of moss in the clearing but the girl was dry and the baby was dry and their things were dry.

Yet despite the noise and the violence of the rainfall it wasn't cold. And between the elongated wet bolts there was a stillness. A sense of the day beginning anew; a refreshment of the fells.

The girl watched the rain. She tried to train her eyes to follow individual drops but they fell too fast and she felt dizzy if she looked at them too long. Then she watched the impact that the drops had on the ground and the trees and the scrub all around her. As she watched the rain rake the land she felt like a creature in a hole.

And she spoke to the baby. She held it up close and bounced it on her chest then she rolled onto her side. She didn't use words – only her thoughts. She shared them with the child and it tried to grab her nose and put its fingers in her mouth. The girl pulled faces and puffed her cheeks and stuck her tongue out and the rain fell. And she spoke to it from inside her head.

They ate berries from the tin can and their lips turned the darkest purple once again.

After a few hours the rain slowed. The drops shrunk and then they stopped altogether and the sky was clear. The tension had gone and when the girl breathed in deep the air smelled sweet.

She took the baby down to the tarn to drink water. The storm had stirred up the silt so it was cloudy and swollen and at the far end there was a new run-off that carved a watery path down the hillside into the next valley. The mountains beyond formed the rim of a giant basin that was jagged against the clear sky. She thought she could see movements up there. Tiny dots walking along the crest; two or three of them so small they might not exist at all.

Anxiety pierced her core and she knew that she would have to move again soon.

They washed and drank and by the time they had walked back to the clearing the sun was setting and soon the day would be over. The girl was wet up to the waist from the grass and bracken.

The baby began to cry so she took a breast out to let it suckle a while. Soon she was dry and sore but the baby had stopped crying so she set it down and gave it her dolly rag to play with.

She pulled the kindling out from underneath the tree and she took the matches the man had given her and lit it. When it was burning she piled bigger sticks on there and then let the fire settle in. She worried about someone seeing the smoke so she let the fire become small and then rolled her potato into the embers with a stick and sat and watched it then she turned to tickle the baby.

She left the potato in the fire for a long time. She put a big stone in there too. She stared into the embers and when she looked up the sky was darker.

When it was fully dark she first rolled the stone out then the potato and set one of the tins on the stone to warm it.

The potato was black. She set it aside to cool a little then she rolled the tin off the stone and set that aside too then when she could wait no longer and her stomach was growling in frustration she opened it. It was broth. It smelled delicious.

She mashed the potato with the spoon and ate some. It was soft and fluffy. She put some on a bracken leaf to cool. The broth wasn't warm near the top so she fed it to the baby who took it hungrily and grabbed for more. She gave it more. A spoon of broth for the baby then potato for herself.

Broth for the baby. Potato for herself.

Then she swapped it and gave some of the cooled potato to the baby and took some soup for herself.

Potato for the baby broth for herself.

Potato then broth. The fire crackling.

Potato then broth. Blowing on the embers.

When the potato was done she folded the skin and put it away for later. They finished the broth. The girl scraped the tin. Contorted her tongue. Lapped at it.

The girl threw bracken onto the fire to kill the glow but not the heat. It started smoking then but she liked the smell it made so left it a while even though it was making her eyes water.

The baby belched.

So did she.

The baby slept.

So did she.

THE DOG PICKED up the scent strong and hauled them up a tree-covered hill near to the end of the lake. The going was steep. The two men conserved their breath.

The dog was panting and salivating. Its wet nose swept the ground and it pulled at its rope until the Poacher untied it and it sprinted on through the trees kicking dirt and dead needles behind it.

They heard it barking up ahead and they quickened their pace. The Poacher withdrew his skinning knife.

When they reached it the dog was crouched low and growling at a man who had pressed himself up against a trunk. Its teeth were showing. Its nostrils flared. Drool suspended. Pendulous.

The Poacher called the dog off but it still kept its eyes on the man and emitted a low curdling growl.

Have you seen a lass? said the Poacher.

The man kept his eyes on the dog.

Well now gentlemen.

Carrying a baby said the Poacher.

The man looked from the Poacher to the Priest. Saw the knife. Saw the Priest's eyes. His strange small teeth. The dog bayed. A low noise. Like rusted metal cogs turning.

The Priest looked beyond him and through the trees to the gaping aperture of a cave.

You're Solomon said the Priest. Aren't you.

The man straightened and sniffed. Shrugged with forced nonchalance.

The Cave Man said the Priest.

I've heard of him said the Poacher. I've heard of you. Didn't think you existed.

I sometimes wonder myself.

Have you seen her? said the Priest. A girl carrying a baby.

Tom Solomon shrugged.

I see many people.

The Poacher spoke. His voice raised into a tone of incredulity.

What – up here in the middle of nowhere? I doubt it.

The child's not hers said the Priest. She stole it.

I'm sure she had her reasons.

So you have seen her said the Poacher.

I never said that my good men. Besides. I'm not someone to pry in another's business. Similarly if you two want to skulk around up here in the woods then skulk away. That's your prerogative. You can be assured I'll say nothing about it to anyone. Discretion is valour.

Don't get smart.

Aye said the Poacher. Smart-arse.

He stepped forward.

How about we have a look around this cave of his Father?

Father? You're a man of the cloth are you asked Solomon. Well now. I'd love to engage you in a debate about the merits of atheism – try and coax you over to my side if you like. Futile I'm sure but a lively theological discussion is always welcome.

Not you as well said the Priest.

As well? I just wondered where you stood on the whole God-is-dead strand of thought.

The Priest moved forwards and spoke.

There'll be no debating.

We're turning over your hovel said the Poacher.

Solomon raised his hands. The dog growled again. A threatening baritone gurgle from deep within its straining gullet.

Gentlemen. I'm afraid entrance is by invite only. If you'd like to schedule a dinner date with my secretary I would be more than happy –

Fucken smart arse tramp said the Poacher as he strode forward and swung the knife in front of Solomon's face. It caught his cheek and opened it up in an instant. He stumbled backwards. The dog growled. Nothing happened for a moment. Then a sheet of blood ran down Tom Solomon's gaping cheek and he gasped. He put his hand to it then looked at the smear across his palm. A flap of skin hung from below his cheek bone. He felt his hanging flesh again then again looked at his hand in disbelief. Through it the men could see a top row of teeth set deep in the jawbone.

The Priest unscrewed the vial from his necklace. He inhaled deeply and he sniffed and then he exhaled and then he spoke

I will leave your flesh on the mountains and fill the valleys with your carcass he said.

Yeah said the Poacher.

I will water the land with what flows from you and the river beds shall be filled with your blood.

The Poacher nodded.

He will and all.

When I snuff you out I will cover the heavens and all the stars will darken said the Priest.

And that'll learn you.

7.

IT WAS IN those moments before the birds start singing when everything seems quiet but when she actually stopped and listened – really listened – that she could hear the sky making a dull flat distant roaring noise like giants were doing battle three valleys over that the girl wriggled out from beneath the tree. She thought the roar of the sky was the true sound of loneliness and could not stay there any longer.

She stood and stretched and then packed up her tin of food her tin opener the empty cans – one slotted inside the other – the spoon and matches. Then she scooped up the baby and started walking.

It was still dark and she didn't yet feel awake. The child felt heavy.

She walked away from the lake and left the hill. She passed the tarn and traversed a series of mini crags that lead down to a long sloping meadow. The meadow stretched all the way along the valley and was dissected by stone walls.

As she crossed it she felt exposed. She felt as if eyes were on her and was relieved when she reached the other side and climbed over a stile and into a wood.

She walked all morning and only stopped once to rest for water and to feed the baby the rest of the bilberries: they had already started to turn in the tin. She pulped them with the spoon so that they were easy to eat.

Then she was at the bottom of an empty dale and there was a stream that was too wide to cross so she walked alongside it for a mile or two. It ran down a series of smoothed stone shelves. Some running fast and violent and others silent and steady slowing only to dip through clear pools. The stream was the run-off from the mountain tops – the confluence of dozens of tiny flows that ran from peat bogs puddles and mossy marshes like broken glass being swept up. It had been reinvigorated by the rainfall from the previous night.

The girl stopped to fill her tin can and take a long drink. The water was cool and tasted of the ancient rounded stones that lined its bed. She drank until she couldn't take any more.

She should have known that the stream would lead to the lake and where streams meet lakes there is often life. She should have noticed the pollarding of the trees that took a more orderly formation around her the further she moved down the valley but she was too busy watching where she put her feet as the path was pitted with pot-holes and divots caused by many centuries of footfall and horse hooves. And though the incline was mild the ground was challenging.

The stream followed a bend and then the girl pulled up as she saw half a mile ahead through the trees some buildings and a road and just beyond them the pebbled shoreline of the narrow end of the lake. She saw people she saw life.

The girl's shoulders slumped. She had walked the long way round from her fallen tree camp. She had taken a wide arc that had led inland. She had walked maybe ten hard miles to cover an easy three.

There were row boats along the shore line and in the distance a wooden pier with a large steam boat beside it. It was bigger than any boat she had ever seen. A union jack flag hung from the brow of it and the name of it was painted along the hull: THE GILDED SWAN. Further along the shore where the water gave way to a flat green flood plain there was a large hotel with a slate roof.

And there were people. There were people everywhere. They were sitting and talking and milling and resting. Civilisation was here with all its laughter and appetites and desires and cruelties.

THE LAKE LOOKED less silver down there. Some of the people were sitting on benches and looking out across the water. Some of them had binoculars while others had picnic hampers and blankets. One man was playing a game with a group of children that involved a stick and a ball and a lot of noise. They all looked happy. There were dogs. The dogs looked happy too.

The girl watched them.

She saw people gather at the pier one or two at a time then they slowly formed themselves into a line and the line walked onto the steamer then the steamer stoked its furnace and pulled away. It sounded a hooter and the noise echoed across the lake. It was the loudest noise the girl had heard in a long time. Louder even than the thunder of the day before.

The girl watched the steamer get smaller and smaller until it moved out past an island and she realised it was *her* island – the one she had looked down upon from a great distance – and then the steamer drifted around the dog-leg bend and it was gone.

Looking at the people by the lake the girl felt more alone than ever. Up on the hill in the trees she hadn't felt this alone. In the darkness of night she had felt cold and sometimes wet and maybe hungry and she worried that the man from the cave wasn't what he seemed and might come back with more people in the night; she had worried that they – Hinckley or the Sisters or worst of all Father – might catch up with her and take her baby away and she worried about the terrible painful things they could do to her. She was more scared of that than anything but she had not felt alone. Now she did. As she watched the people with their sandwiches and their flasks and their laughter and their dogs the girl felt more alone than all those nights in St. Mary's. More alone than a dozen Christmas days without presents or smiles or family or song.

She wished that she had never seen the people by the lake. She wished she had stayed up on the hill or was on her island or in a cave. Anywhere but here on the edge of other people's lives.

Some of the buildings near the water were houses. Small stone houses. Others were shops selling provisions and postcards and clothes for walking and one was a tea room.

It looked like a popular place.

The girl wanted to go down the hill and out of the trees and across the road. She wanted to push through the gate and walk down to the people. Down to the shore. She would sit and rest a while and say hello what a nice day it is have you had a nice walk and people would reply. They would say yes lovely thank you isn't the lake beautiful aren't the hills beautiful isn't the sky beautiful and then they would invite her to come and join them on their blanket because there was plenty of tea and sandwiches and fruit cake for everyone. And then they'd say oh what a lovely child you have and the girl would smile and say thank you and they would say it's very well behaved and then ask how old and she would say oh just a few months and they would say they're special when they're that young and the girl would smile and reply yes yes they are and they would say you should cherish every second because before you know it they'll be grown and gone and the girl would say oh yes I will I mean I am I do and she would take another sip of tea. But when she thought now about the baby growing and becoming something else – first a wee one then an adolescent then a young adult who was no longer reliant on her to feed and clothe and protect it – she felt an even greater chasm of sadness open up inside her. A bottomless dark dank well bigger and deeper and more intense than ever. Because without the child who relied upon her she did not know if she would exist any longer. So long as there was this responsibility – this bond – life had a purpose. But without the child she would be back to being what she was before.

A person without purpose. Nothing. A non entity.

The girl turned away from the lake. Away from the people with their hampers and balls and dogs. And away from the tea-room that she so desperately wanted to go in but knew she couldn't.

People might know about her down there. Word had likely spread. It always did.

Keep your tongue from evil and your lips from speaking lies.

Because that's what they were like. People. They gossiped. They celebrated the misfortune of others. They loved to hate as much as they loved their other sins and they always needed targets. That hate had to go somewhere otherwise it would chew them up inside and make them take a hard look at themselves and no-one likes to do that because they rarely like what they see.

Yes. The girl knew exactly what they were like. She may not have been out in the world but she had seen and heard enough of people to know the cruelty they were capable of.

The girl wished that she could go into one of the shops to find a newspaper because although she couldn't read they might have a photograph of her in there and then she would know if they were on to her.

Of course they were on to her.

Who was she kidding.

Of course they were.

Who would let a girl steal a baby without doing something about it?

No-one normal.

And if it did make it into the paper the photograph would be old. It would be the only one she had ever had taken.

It was when she had arrived at St Mary's. That very first day. They had a man come round. A man with a big camera and a tripod and a moustache. He made her sit straight-backed on a stool and told her not to smile. Said it wasn't that type of photo whatever that meant. Said it was for their records.

They combed her hair and gave her clean clothes and told her not to fidget or she'd get a strap. She sat confused. Rigid. A statue of a scared child.

That was a long time ago now. How long? Long enough for her body to grow and swell and develop new scents and her features to cast new shadows across her face. Once she was a slight thing but now she had filled out. A decade's work. She had lost her freckles and her shape had changed. She had hips now – and full breasts and hair growing on different parts.

And she bled. She had never bled back then when the photograph had been taken but now it seemed to happen all the time – damn near every few weeks. She couldn't understand it. She wondered if something was wrong inside; that maybe things weren't built right in there and that perhaps she was dying and then it wouldn't matter if they caught up with her because it was likely that she didn't have long left anyway.

Death didn't scare her though. Not at all; death brings peace and silence.

The only thing that worried her was the bairn – the thought of it without someone who fed it and clothed it and carried it and protected it from thunder and farmers and wild animals and more than anything loved it; who would love it more than anyone had ever loved any single thing. Her. The new mother.

She never did see that photograph.

After it had been taken she had climbed down from the chair and gone to the camera and waited for the man to open it so she could see the picture inside but he slapped her hand away and said that these things took time and money and what did she think – that he was some sort of magician or something?

Stupid lass he'd said.

Stupid lass.

THE POACHER USED a fistful of grass to wipe the blade of his hunting knife then he inserted it into the rabbit's anus and cut along its belly. In two more moves he had disembowelled it and thrown the guts to Perses who wolfed them down then looked to him for more. His huge tongue painting a circle of saliva and viscera around its nose.

With one hand he pared along the rabbit's frame and with the other he tugged at its pelt.

Isn't it a sin Father he asked.

The Priest was sitting on a stone and poking at the fire with a stick.

What?

You know. I hardly want to say it.

The Poacher dropped his voice.

Murder he said.

What do you think?

I do believe killing is bad.

The Priest raised his head from the fire and looked at him.

Yet you kill animals every day.

That's different.

Trapping and snaring and shooting and hooking isn't sinful?

It's different.

Is it?

They're just animals.

And humans aren't?

Humans are humans. But animals are animals.

That's your justification? Animals are animals.

Some of them are pests Father.

So are some humans.

What does God say about all this?

Why don't you ask him.

Ask him?

Yes.

How?

Through prayer.

Prayer.

Yes.

But I'm not Godly Father. You know that.

The Poacher held the rabbit aloft and inspected it. He ran his forearm across his brow. Its eyes were brilliant stone and its narrow front teeth long and inverted. Tinged brown. He pressed at its snout and checked its mouth then dropped it.

You say you aren't but yet you ask God's opinion said the Priest.

I asked your opinion on what God would think.

That's the same thing.

Not quite.

Yet you still seek God's approval.

I'm just worried I'm going to the other place.

The other place.

Down there. Hell like.

You believe in hell?

Of course. Don't you Father?

We make our own hells.

That's a strange answer.

It's a truthful answer said the Priest.

So am I going there Father? When I die like.

That's up to Him to decide.

How. How will he decide?

It depends how well your have served Him in life.

The Priest reached into his bag and took out a small mirror and checked his hair. He gently palmed it into place.

Served him Father?

Yes. It depends on whether you have done His work.

What about you?

What about me?

Are you going there?

The Priest unscrewed his vial and spooned some powder into each nostril. He made a snorting noise at the back of his throat.

I told you he said. That's up for Him to decide.

What happened back there –

What happened back there will remain a secret if you know what's good for you said the Priest as he carefully palmed the vial's stopper back into place.

Heck said the Poacher. I'm not going to be bragging about it down the Shoulder Of Mutton Father. I'm not stupid.

It happened. It was God's judgement. A sacrifice for a greater good.

Would you do the same to the girl though?

I wasn't thinking about the girl. I was merely mopping up the mess you created.

The Poacher ran his stick into the skinned rabbit's mouth and pushed it out through its back end. Then he rested it on the Y-shaped spit handles that he had cleaved and then driven into the ground either side of the fire.

By making a bigger mess? he said quietly. I just hope we don't get found out. I only meant to scare him a bit. A little or cut or two. A new smile to remember us by. You being a Priest I didn't think that you'd be so –

Look said the Priest. What is more valuable: the life of an innocent baby stolen from its parents and good God-fearing people at that – members of the community – people who contribute to the order of things or the life of a useless old troglodyte who sees no harm in taking the Lord's name in vain because he doesn't even believe in the Lord? A man who is of no use to society or the advancement of civilisation because he chooses to live like a beast in a mountain cave and whose worthless life is nearly over anyway? If Solomon was a good Christian he would have offered to help us in our search. But as it is he chose to oppose us. The Book of the Wisdom Of Solomon says: as gold in the furnace he proved them and as sacrificial offerings he took them to himself. It is already written.

Book Of Solomon. I didn't see him with no book.

My point is we are just fulfilling a deed as prophesied.

What's prophesised?

Predicted said the Priest. It means predicted. Foretold.

You mean this was meant to happen all along? You looked like the devil himself back there by that cave. You can't tell me that was planned Father.

I took the action that the situation demanded said the Priest.

But we've still not found the bairn.

We got information out of the old man didn't we? We know we're on the right path. We know she's been through here. The girl.

The Poacher adjusted the rabbit on the spit. He held it firm as he pulled the stick part of the way out of the centre of it and then he pushed it in again.

Seems like he had to pay a high price he said.

He'll not be missed. But that baby has everything to live for. We'll find them.

You think? said the Poacher.

I know.

Because it was prophesised?

The Priest cleared his throat and looked into the fire. He licked his thin lips and ran his tongue over his small square teeth then smoothed his fine auburn hair into place again. His fingers felt electric on his scalp. Charged. The flames wavered and fluttered. He was entranced; his gaunt face illuminated.

Because it was prophesised Father the Poacher asked again.

Because I just know.

THAT NIGHT THE girl crouched behind a wall on the fells and tried to sleep.

She had left the lake and the people with their picnics and their games and their dogs behind. She needed to put distance between them so she had climbed the next fell over. She had walked all day and drank from streams and made the baby drink too. It fidgeted and howled and scratched at her back.

When the lake was a small mirror reflecting the sky in the distance she stopped. Her legs ached and she felt the rise and swell of a blister on the ball of her other foot. She set the baby free and let it crawl through the long grass and for a few minutes it was quiet and it seemed happy but when it picked up sheep droppings and started to stuff them into its mouth the girl had to knock them out of its hand and then it started crying again. It howled harder and louder than before. It cried for an hour and it didn't stop. The girl didn't do anything about it. She was too tired. She leaned against the wall and closed her eyes and blocked everything out.

When she opened them the baby was still crying so she took the final tin of food and opened it with the tin opener. It had beans in it. The colour of the beans was vivid and almost unreal and they smelled strongly of salt and sugar. She hungrily ate a few spoonfuls without even giving any to the baby and almost instantly felt some strength returning.

The girl fed the bairn and it gulped each mouthful down and then opened up for more. It was a hungry little bird sitting in the world's biggest nest.

She poured water in its mouth to help fill it up more quickly and drank more herself; she wanted to create an illusion of satisfaction. She wanted to trick their stomachs into being full.

She also wanted fire and shelter and warmth but she was on an open fell side and couldn't risk fire. The best she could hope for was to find another bracken patch and crawl into it.

In the far distance the village by the lake was now just a cluster of tiny specks. There was no movement and it was hard to believe that there was life there. Behind her the mountain loomed large.

She turned the bairn loose again and let it crawl and roll in the grass while she took in the view. From up here she could see three different valleys feeding down to the lake and make out part of a fourth just beyond a series of long meandering tree plantations. It was on a dense outcrop at the lower end of one of these that she had slept in the night before.

Each valley was different in length but similar in colour and creation. The middle valley was a very popular area for walkers. Walkers brought money. Money rung changes. The Lakelands were changing. She had seen that down by the lake.

As she rested she watched the sky. She watched the clouds slide overhead and she listened to the light breeze in the grass and she observed the baby as it discovered the world for the first time. With each slow movement of the eye a new experience.

The girl stood. She was unstable on her legs. They were weak and unsure. She scanned the fell above her with squinted eyes. She shielded them with one hand. The sun was moving behind the mountains. She couldn't picture winter.

A few hundred yards uphill she thought she could make out a path. An old horse trail perhaps and before the trail she could make out another shape on the fell side. A sheepfold.

She picked up the bairn in her arms and walked up the hill towards it. Her thighs were screaming now and she felt like she could drop but she continued straight up the hill for ten minutes then across to the right for ten minutes. She walked on grass. This was grazing territory. There were few boulders.

Gasps filled her ears and her chest was thumping. Sweat patched on sore skin and the afternoon moon looked misshapen. Crooked. She could go no further.

The fold was empty. Dirty white wool matted its corners and the trodden ground was littered with the familiar scatterings of compressed dung pellets. But there were no sheep to be seen. It was summer and the days were long – they would be higher up the fell. They only used the folds when they had to.

The girl slumped down against the wall with the baby still cradled in her arms her organs aching dry stone dehydration. Constipated. Disoriented. Tongue stuck and mute trapped.

She slept.

INTERESTING WHAT THAT tramp said about the death of God said the Poacher.

When the Priest didn't respond he continued: like I was just thinking how maybe it won't always be that you Godly folk are the ones that are running things and how they say that science will one day replace religion.

Do they.

What do you reckon to that though?

Do I look like a man who places stock in science as a philosophical construct said the Priest. As something to evince faith in its followers? Do I strike you as a Darwinist?

Too many long words there Father.

There's no point talking to you.

A man shouldn't be a book learner to have an opinion though. My father taught me that.

Remind me what your father does.

Same as me.

A thief.

No – not a thief. A hunter. A farmer of sorts.

You're no more a farmer than the foxes you hunt.

Don't hunt foxes unless I'm paid to sniffed the Poacher. Might be that a farmer's sick of having his hens got and might be that he wants my help with that. But foxes are no use to my pot. Ever tried eating fox meat? I wouldn't recommend that. I'd sooner eat a flank of Perses than try that again. No. Plant-eating creatures make for the best meat. Everyone knows that.

That wasn't my point.

See me and some of the boys were having a blether about this not but two or three days gone.

This will be good.

And a lad called Hughie reckons that damn near everything that is written in the great Book about like the beginnings of man and Adam and Eve and all of that has now been like disproved by scientists and college men and dinosaur bones and fossils.

The Priest snorted at this. Said nothing. They walked on.

Old Hughie reckoned on those dinosaurs being some fifty thousand years old or maybe more but in the great book they reckon it says God made everything only like a few thousand years ago. Now how do you account for that? Seems to me that someone somewhere along the way is wrong so it got me thinking about how it all comes to choice in opinion. Do we believe in the thigh bone of a creature the size of a house or some words on a page that most of us don't much have the time or inclination to read?

When you say inclination you mean ability says the Priest. Because if more of you learned to read then you might have picked up Darwin's *Origin of Species* which covers exactly these matters at fatuous and blasphemous length and after whose reading any sane man of faith would agree that this current fashion for God-denial is exactly that: a fashion.

So how do you explain bones older than the great book?

I wouldn't usually waste my words but since you ask I can explain it easily said the Priest: they are God's test.

How's that like?

Because everything on this planet was created by God. Every speck of dirt every towering mountain every idiot poacher.

That's your opinion –

Shut up I'm talking now. Everything – *every thing* – was made by His hand. This is a fact. An old bone means nothing except that we cannot possibly understand all His ways because His will is far greater than we can ever imagine. It's really very simple: the bone is a test. Do we let our faith crumble the moment we cannot explain everything we see and hear and smell – the moment we first have doubts – or do we strengthen our resolve and accept him fully and totally into our hearts?

The Poacher shook his head.

I don't know Father. Hughie reckoned –

Hughie is – I do not doubt – a faithless idiot an illiterate and a drunk. Charles Darwin meanwhile has readily and publicly denied the existence of God so how on earth do you suppose we are to believe a single word he writes. Of course on his deathbed he will repent and see sense. He'll come back to God – you'll see. And this absurd trend will pass. I will however concede one point and one point only to Mr Darwin: the strong will indeed survive. On this point I agree but with the addendum that only those strong *in faith* will survive. Faith and will and dedication to a higher purpose are all that matters. Now – come on – I've wasted enough energy on this.

8.

IT WAS A miniscule dot to begin with. An orange apparition suspended in the night.

Her first sleepy thought: this is it. They have found me. They have come with torches.

But it was something else – something alive – and it was moving and it felt wrong so she rose and walked towards it propelled by instinct and nullified by the tightening anxiety that had woken her in the first place.

The girl moved towards the apparition. She stumbled many times but she never fell.

There was movement around the glow – shapes were shooting upwards and wafted by an upended flapping flag of rising fire. Then she heard the noises and quickened her pace. The golden phoenix of flames was hissing and roaring in baritone. Cutting through the crackle and bluster of the heat were other sounds: a panicked bray followed by something guttural and desperate. The sound of metamorphosis.

She was running now. The baby bouncing and crying.

There was an opacity to the flames but when the girl stepped down between some boulders and over the scattered remnants of a tumbledown wall she saw through the flickers a smallholding building painted cadmium orange by heat.

A barn was burning. A barn and everything in it.

Chaos clattered against its wavering walls as she slowed first to a jog then a standstill. There was a fuss of clicking hooves and heads and limbs banging and barging in an attempt at a forced exit. Desperate movements. Futile.

The braying and screaming cut right through her and turned her cold as the contents of the barn struggled to get out. Then the roof took hold and the fire was amplified. She clasped the baby to her chest.

Embers danced on the updrafts. Tiny gobbets; moths taking flight.

Inside the horses howled and the barn began to cave in on itself as burning beams drew terracotta tangents against the blackness of the hill. Diagonal sweeping lines traced slow-motion crescents. She was surprised at the speed at which it fell and how the noises from the animals seemed to carry on long into the night even after they had ceased to make them.

Whatever was in there was no longer animate.

The baby screamed.

Then there were voices: one high and hysterical the other low and acute. Figures beyond the fire. The girl stepped backwards in fear that the diminishing flames might in their final illuminations offer her up as a culprit to these people.

For wickedness burneth as the fire: it shall devour the briers and thorns and shall kindle in the thickets of the forest and they shall mount up like the lifting up of smoke.

The people who arrived were much too late and they knew it. Their hurried movements slowed and the buckets in their hands fell by their sides and then they just stood there and the girl was glad that they hadn't heard what she had heard – that tortured cry of the horses as they hissed and charred with their manes ablaze their tails already gone and caruncles burning bright across their backs. Then in those final moments before they had fallen: the sounds of skin scorching and eyeballs popping pain giving way to resolution; their instincts not programmed to wonder why this was happening.

COOKED MEAT. CHARRED and blackened. Great lumps of it.

The burnt horses were still smouldering at dawn when the girl returned to take another look. She saw their cremains in amongst the fallen beams and the rubble of collapsed masonry. They were barely recognisable now as creatures once capable of great feats of endurance and stamina and loyalty.

What was left of their limbs looked like roots burnt out. One creature was on its back with its gnarled legs reaching for the sky and its trunk shattered and exposed like an exploded safe. Its pelt had burnt away and beneath it the flesh was seared. The mane and tail long gone but the skull intact. Teeth still strong and white remained set in its jaw-bone.

All eye sockets were empty. Hooves were molten and sticky. Fetlocks contorted.

The smell hung in the air. All that meat. Sweet and nauseating. Hunks and flanks of it. Hocks and shanks. Sides still smoking.

Yet as the girl surveyed this field of death sculptures – this open sepulchre on the smouldering hillside – she found her mouth watering at the scent on the breeze. Her body craved the protein. She felt drunk with hunger.

She shifted the baby from one hip to another. She looked at the horses solidified by flame and doused by buckets of water scooped from trough and dub. She smelled the air one final time.

No.

Could she?

She couldn't.

She couldn't do it.

She turned and began to walk.

THIS GIRL SAID the Poacher. She must be pretty special.

She's not special replied the Priest. She's not special at all.

Days we've been out here and you tell me she's not special said the Poacher.

That's what I said.

I don't understand Father.

You're not meant to understand – just guide.

It just seems like you're going to a lot of trouble that's all. You don't strike me as the outdoor type.

What said the Priest. Because I'm not malodorous in oilskins like you.

So why the big fuss?

No big fuss.

No big fuss he says. Me I can bivvy out for weeks at a time. It's no sweat off my back. The sky's the only blanket I need. But you – you I suspect have got other things you can be doing. I've seen them churches. Right luxurious they are. Hot meals cooked for you and your washing done. Nice little income too I'd wager. No traipsing through mud and middens to do a hard day's work for your lot Father.

I don't recall seeing you at service on Sunday said the Priest. Or any day.

I've told you Father: not my thing.

And as far as I'm aware a hard day's work is about as familiar to you as the works of Aeschylus.

What's Aeschylus?

My point is stealing animals from landowners is not exactly virtuous. The one who is unwilling to work shall not eat. Thessalonians 3:10.

But that's where your Bible is wrong isn't it said the Poacher. I don't go hungry. Me or mine.

Let the thief no longer steal, but rather let him labour. Ephesian 4:28.

Sometimes you talk like you don't have a mind of your own Father. It's like you're scared of saying something un-Godly.

I'm not scared spat the Priest. Scared is the last thing that I am.

THE OLD CART horse track kept the girl high on the fell side. For a while she walked upstream in parallel with a river that ran the length of the valley bottom then coiled and bent through a series of silted oxbow turns made shallow by banks of grainy sediment before splaying out into the lake end. The widening fan of pebbles and rocks washed down from the waterfalls of the fells was visible from high up above.

But the lake with its walkers and day trippers was long behind her now as she headed deeper into the mountains. What lay beyond was a magnet drawing her on.

It was a mild day and the breeze kept her cool. She stopped to rest by the trackside and unfolded the potato skin from her pocket. It was creased and lined like an old parchment. The girl gnawed on it and pulped the dry skin as best she could then gave it to the baby. She only swallowed two small lumps for herself.

Then when it was gone the girl undid her top and took out a tit and let the baby suckle. She was sore and arid and it took many minutes of the baby chewing and tugging before a small amount of watery milk trickled out. That which the baby didn't take she caught with a finger then ran it back up her breast and into its mouth. The baby suckled long after the milk had ended. Its gums clicking on her swollen gland.

She felt too exposed on the fell side like this. The grass was trimmed short from a summer's grazing and anyone could see her from a mile away. The girl preferred the cover of thicket or spinney. Any terrain into which she could merge and move. She left the track and began to head down hill with her feet sliding on the sheep-shorn grass.

SO THIS GIRL.

Yes.

She came from St. Mary's. She was orphaned – is that right?

More or less.

And you and the Sisters raised her.

With God's guidance yes.

For her entire life.

For most of her life.

And then you turned her out.

No. We didn't turn her out. She came of age and we found a place for her in a good home in the town. Church people. The Hinckleys. We had her doing honest work for honest pay – something you wouldn't understand.

Looking after this bairn.

Amongst other things – yes.

And then she ran off and took Hinckley's bairn with her.

We've been through all this.

And here we are hot-footing it after her.

Yes.

And she's a dummy.

Yes.

She doesn't speak.

So they say.

So they say Father?

Yes. So they say.

But she hears alright doesn't she? said the Poacher.

What point are you trying to make?

There's plenty of others that could go after her Father.

Others?

Police. Or them in power. The authorities.

And the Church does not occupy a position of power? countered the Priest. She was in my care.

I thought you said she was with the Hinckleys now.

She is but –

But you're involved in other ways.

Involved?

I'm just speculating Father.

It's not your place to speculate.

I mean it looks pretty odd from where I'm sitting. It's almost as if you don't want this lass going out in the world –

She has abducted a child. A child. That is a crime.

You don't care about the child though Father said the Poacher. That's not what this is about is it?

Well what is it about then?

I don't know Father. Secrets?

Secrets?

Yes secrets said the Poacher. I think she is full of them. Your secrets.

Is that right.

Yes.

Do you want to know what I think? said the Priest. I'll tell you: I think you're as thick as pig excrement and twice as smelly. I think you're just an ignorant peasant who's no better than the fox that sneaks in and kills the chickens at night.

That right.

That's right. You have no idea what you are talking about.

Funny how you're getting upset though isn't it Father smiled the Poacher unfazed. Like I said: this girl. She must be pretty special the way you're chasing across the land like this and not getting them that's in charge involved. The authorities and all that. Keeping it a secret. All hush-hush. It's like she's an escaped prisoner that's got something of yours.

No-one was forcing –

The Poacher was emboldened now. He interrupted the Priest.

Or maybe it's her that's yours. Maybe you feel she belongs to you to do with what you want. And maybe she's not such a dummy. Maybe she's got a tongue in her mouth and a headful of secrets to spill out. Secrets about things most un-Godly. Am I right?

You have no idea.

Am I right?

This is a pointless conversation.

I'm right though aren't I Father?

You know nothing of charity said the Priest. This girl has been given the best of the church's charity. She has been given the fullest of care and attention and learning. And this is how she repays us.

Sounds like you're after revenge Father. Revenge or ownership of what's yours. But what do I know I'm just an ignorant peasant.

The thing about you is –

I think I've had enough of the talking for now Father.

You don't just say these things and then –

Think like maybe I need to go and catch me some more food like.

The Poacher showed the Priest his broad back.

TARGETS. SHE SET herself them. Attainable targets. Get to that crag that's taller than the others and the reward will be a rest. Five minutes. Get to that sharp rock on the skyline. The hole in the wall. The bone-bare tree.

And don't look back. Because behind you is the past and that is fixed; that has happened that cannot be changed but in front is a future waiting to be shaped. Options were becoming conceivable for the first time.

So she walked. To the sharp rock on the skyline. To the hole in the wall. To the tree stripped of its bark and now bone white like a sheep that's gone down a gulley.

Despite the fear and despite the fatigue and the thirst and the hunger she saw that to another person living another life these hills could be beautiful.

Squinting in the afternoon sun it was as if she saw the countryside for the first time as until now all she had known was walls and dorms and beds and darkness. Repetition and restriction and exploitation. The outdoors had been beyond her reach.

And as she passed through the wild landscape the girl felt the landscape passing through her. She was the filter for it. Every pebble every bracken patch. Every fallen tree or fold. It passed through her as much as she passed through it. And it fed her. Energised her. Kept her going. In these fleeting moments she felt nature working as an ally and this gave her hope.

THE SUN CAUGHT something on the fell side above them – something glinting – and the Poacher said here look at that and pointed at it with the stick he was using and the Priest said what is it and the Poacher said I don't know but I'll find out right enough. He broke off from the path and walked uphill and when he got closer the sun was no longer reflecting off the brass plating of the camping stove but he was close enough to see it so walked on and when he got there he picked it up and turned in his hand. Puzzled he turned it upside down and shook it and then turned it back again and began to try and unscrew its various components. He held it up by the handle and let the late afternoon sun shine on it again and downhill the Priest was waving his arms to get his attention and then he was shouting something through cupped hands but the Poacher ignored him and studied his precious find again.

THE GIRL PICKED her way carefully aware that even a minor injury like a turned ankle could be catastrophic for both of them.

The base of the mountain bulged and there was coverage in which she was able to sit and rest. Once or twice as she blundered through the undergrowth she startled rabbits who burrowed beneath it. Sometimes three or four of them at a time darted out not more than a few feet in front of her but always just out of reach. If she had twine she could set snares but there was no twine.

Then she remembered the serrated edge of the tin lid and she took it from her pocket and ran her thumb along it. It was still sharp. She left the gorse and carried on walking down to the next dry stone wall that marked the top end of a farmstead. She scanned the ground for a stick. There were very few trees.

She finally found a knotted length of larch branch that ran to shoulder height.

The girl carried it back into the bracken then took the baby from her back and began to pick the needles from the stem. Then she sharpened one end with the improvised blade. The wood was hard and she had to scrape and scratch at it but after a few minutes she had fashioned a crude spear with a tip so pointed it looked too fine and ornamental to kill any living thing.

She climbed higher up the slope and left the baby sleeping in the shade then found a clearing where she crouched with spear poised. Ready to strike. It was only twenty feet or so across – a space where the bracken had not taken.

Minutes passed. The girl's thighs began to burn from the strain of her hunkered position. Then she heard the sound of crying on the breeze. The baby. She ignored it. More minutes passed before the girl stood and stretched. The bracken was too vast and dense to expect a rabbit to appear in this small clearing. She turned to walk back to the baby and as she tramped through the tangle a blur of white crossed the corner of her vision. She spun round as a disturbed rabbit shot past her and made a break for it. The girl pulled the spear back then aimed for a second and flung it as hard as she could. It hit the ground flat and bounced as the rabbit darted off at a tangent into the dark safety of the soil.

She stared at the spear for some time. The hope of earlier had given way to hopelessness and she felt foolish to have felt that nature was her ally; that the landscape somehow was on her side and would provide when she needed provisions.

She hadn't even broken soil.

THE CHILD'S CHEEKS were flushed red and scratched from its lolling in the stubble and the fallen fronds. It was howling and when the girl picked it up it violently grabbed for her breast with a curled fist but this time she knew that nothing would come. She pressed the back of her hand to its cheek and felt it burning up. The child's eyes searched the girl's face for an answer to its increasing feelings of hunger and heat and thirst but she could offer nothing. Not even water. She too was thirsty. She had to move.

Now.

The herd were masticating and swatting flies with their whip-like tails in the languid afternoon heat as the girl rested her hands on the top of the lower farmstead wall and slowly placed her chin on top of them.

They were dappled Shorthorns as creamy in colour as their produce. Their undersides painted darker with dust. Some of them were noisily chewing cud and letting their jaws work in circular motions. Others stood staring into the middle distance with blank long-lashed eyes. Three or four laid prone.

She checked for a bull but there was none to be seen. The grazing meadow ran out the back of a farm with a small milking parlour up where the mountain levelled out to this smallholding.

The girl waited and watched for a farmer or a herdsman. She picked out one of the smaller cows that had shown little movement for minutes. She knew she would have to be quick.

When you reap the harvest of your land do not reap to the very edges of your field or gather the gleanings of your harvest. Leave them for the poor and the alien.

She penned the child in with large stones and covered it in bracken then climbed the wall. Her movements were slow and considered. She tried to stay calm and relaxed as she walked directly to the cow that she had chosen. When she reached it and gently patted its great trunk and felt the foam that was seeping from its hide the cow turned its head and considered her with a look of disaffection.

She made sure that the creature stood between her and the milking parlour then she knelt and reached for one of the teats that dangled from its distended udder. She pulled and squeezed but nothing happened. She did it again and a sharp thin jet of milk squirted out of its pin-hole teat end and soaked her hand. The girl placed the tin can beneath the udder and massaged the thick stubby teat again. When it was a quarter full she couldn't wait any longer and she stepped back and drank the milk straight down. It was warm and strong and velvety. A not-yet-clotted coating for her dry throat. The cow adjusted its footing but showed no signs of anxiety so she squatted again and milked it until the can was two thirds full. Each squeeze of the teat was a gamble against her freedom; she could wait no longer. She turned and briskly walked back to the wall. She placed the tin on top then climbed over and then returned to the baby who was howling again.

The girl sat it up in the crook of her arm and shoulder and it drank thirstily. She kept stopping so that the bairn didn't get sick. It stopped crying. She took a sip or two for herself but fed the baby until all the milk was gone. The girl sat and savoured the buttery aftertaste. The child vomited then fell asleep.

DUST WAS DANCING over mossy humps and rotted stumps.

The girl reached the forest by evening just as the sun was sitting low. She was close to collapse.

There was a boggy patch of mulched leaves so she followed this dark patch uphill deeper into the darkness until she found the trickle of running water that had fed it. She drank for a long time then picked twigs and needles from her mouth and doused the babies' head and made it drink.

The baby was subdued. She freed it from the wrappings and let it crawl. It lay on its back and quietly gurgled.

The forest felt like a dead location. Semi-submerged logs rose from the earth like the bows of sunken ships resurfacing or the limbs of mossy creatures rising from the leaf-covered loam and old overgrown logging trails appeared ghostly in the absence of industry. It was a dusty cluttered place where even in high summer fallen branches appeared skeletal: unfurling ribbons of bark peeled back from the tree trunks by the force of their own tightening membranes.

The air was dense and pungent; the aroma of the ancient weald, one of rot and decay. Between the trees and the black marais small stagnant hollows rank with sulphur held the remains of a thousand years of fallen creatures. Putrefaction and petrification occurred here. There was little sign of human visitation. The trees were birdless. Ultimate silence prevailed.

Thou makest darkness – and it is night.

Here the girl slept. Spent.

A DRONE. DEEP and monotonous. Sonorous and broad.

It pierced her fitful sleep. It soundtracked her anxiety and made her fearful.

A dark bombination.

Not yet awake but already walking she gravitated towards it. She left the bairn to follow it. In the moment she wasn't even aware it was in her possession was not conscious of her surroundings or predicament; only the pull of the reedy thrum. Through the woods she went.

The drone thickened her sleepy fug. The girl walked some way blindly stepping over trunks and roots. Then the trees were ending and barbs were piercing her skin but she was immune to the pinheads of pain. She stopped and parted branches and there was a stream running over smooth round stones and across the water she saw people. Fifteen or more. She stooped out of sight. They had a look of closeness about them. A genetic continuity.

The drone came from a boxy instrument that a hunched man was playing. One hand held down keys while the other pumped air into the back of it. He wrestled with it as if it contained a demon. He was grimly determined as he squeezed out a threnody to the unseen dead.

The stream was shallow but an eddy had been sectioned off to form a side pool only a few feet across and little more than two feet deep. The water was clear. Mountain water. A slow shift of glass.

The crowd were focused on a girl in a white smock who was standing knee deep in the water. She had red cheeks and red wet lips. Around her age – maybe younger. Next to her was a man in a dark robe. A priest. He had a book in his hand and he was reading from it. Another Father.

The girl could just make out his words above the drone from the harmonium and the trill of the water flowing over the rocks.

Be strong in the Lord and in the strength of his might he intoned. Put on the whole armour of God that you may be able to stand against the schemes of the devil. For we do not wrestle against flesh and blood but against the rulers against the authorities against the cosmic powers over this present darkness against the spiritual forces of evil in the heavenly places. Therefore take up the whole armour of God that you may be able to withstand in the evil day and having done all to stand firm.

A murmur ran through the assembled crowd. A couple of them nodded. She thought of Father. Of course she did.

Stand therefore having fastened on the belt of truth and having put on the breastplate of righteousness and as shoes for your feet having put on the readiness given by the gospel of peace.

The priest guided the girl in the smock deeper into the water. She could see that the girl was younger than she first thought – at the dawn of her body turning – and she looked scared. The water rose above her knees and dampened her thighs. He moved round her so that he was facing the people on the bank side. None of them were smiling. The waterline rose and soaked her robe. Made it transparent.

The priest continued proselytizing and his voice raised louder than before. The girl watched from the tangle at the edge of the woods. She barely dared to breathe.

In circumstances take up the shield of faith with which you can extinguish all the flaming darts of the evil one he recited. And take the helmet of salvation and the sword of Spirit – which is the sword of God – praying at all times in the Spirit with all prayer and supplication.

Another murmur of approval. The girl in the water shivered. Her pubic hair could be seen through the cloying cloth of the smock. The man put his hand on her head.

To that end keep alert with all perseverance. Making supplication for all the saints and also for me that words may be given to me in opening my mouth boldly to proclaim the mystery of the gospel for which I am an ambassador in chains – that I may declare it boldly – as I ought to speak.

At the edge of the trees the girl lost her footing and fell back in the barbed furze with a howl. The drone stopped dead. The priest ceased his recitation and looked up. Collectively the crowd turned towards her. The young girl in the smock looked up. Their eyes searched the trees for the source of the noise. She went cold with fear beneath their gaze.

Who's there said the priest and took unsteady steps further out into the water. Who goes there?

The girl turned and ran as fast as she could back into the wood. Her torso led and her legs followed and her arms cartwheeled to propel her onwards.

She sprinted back to the baby and snatched it up along with her scant belongings: the matches the empty can and the tin opener. She ran. She ducked timber limbs and leapt the tangled roots that crawled across the forest floor like monstrous ligneous snakes. Branches thrashed at her face scratching and snagging in her hair but she didn't slow until her lungs were burning and she tasted bile in her throat. She gasped for breath. She drank it in and held a hand to the mouth of the bairn whose face was souring and darkening and screwing up like newspaper thrown onto a fire. Soft gums nipped at the edge of her hand but she held it there and willed the baby into silence. Forced it to breathe through its tiny mucus-encrusted nose. Then the girl found a tree and leaned against it. Chest heaving and burning. She pushed herself into the ground and wished the soil beneath would take her.

IN ALL SERIOUSNESS man to man like – where is it you're from Father? Your family I mean. Where did you grow up.

The Priest sighed.

Why? he said. Why do you need to know this?

The Poacher and the Priest and the dog were moving side by side through the trees. Strips of sunlight crossed their faces then shadows then sunlight again. The Poacher had taken a stick and was whittling it with his knife as they walked. The gas stove that he had found was stashed in his inside pocket.

It's not a need Father he said. It's not a need at all. I'm just asking. Just trying to get another angle on all this.

The Priest didn't reply.

Is it a religious family you're from? Is that how you became a Priest? Was it decided young like?

You ask a lot of questions.

Someone once told me the best way to make conversation was to ask questions Father.

Maybe I don't want to make conversation.

I thought it'd take our mind off things.

Maybe I don't want to make my mind off things.

Stop us thinking like.

Only a fool would want to stop thinking.

Are you saying I'm a fool Father? That's not the first insult you've sent my way today.

The brain is a gift from God. You should use it. An idle mind is the devil's workshop.

They walked on.

Alright then said the Priest. What about you?

Ask me anything you like.

Is it a poaching family you're from. Is that how you became a poacher. Was it decided young?

The Poacher smiled.

Very good Father. I see what you did there – turned my questions back on me. But since you ask: yes it's a poaching family I'm from. My father hunted and his father before him. I remember when I was a nipper –

I'm not interested in your banal *Bildungsroman* snapped the Priest.

Minutes passed in silence. Finally the Poacher spoke.

You know I was just thinking that right around now Father I feel like I could drink up a cup of coffee. Do you take coffee?

Unless you've got some there's no point in asking.

Yes. Coffee would be good.

You don't understand do you?

Understand what Father?

Just keep walking.

Understand what Father?

....

Understand what Father?

....

9.

EVERYTHING HAD TAKEN on a yellow hue as if a jaundiced veil had been drawn. The landscape had a flatness to it. The mountains stood tall and the cirrus clouds streaked across the sky high above them but it was as if distance had diminished and perspective no longer existed. The clouds now appeared within reach. Everything appeared within reach. A flat collage of dead shapes. The girl's head swam from the wanting. The hunger. The yellow tones turned ochre. Her body seemed to separate at the waist. Her upper lip was wet. She wiped it and licked her finger. Tasted salt.

Thirst and hunger. Hunger and thirst. Both were doing battle and making the girl delirious. Toying with her perceptions. Her legs and arms were hollow. Her tongue torrid. Her fingers trembled and tried to take flight. Vision skewed. Sounds bent. Fear.

She needed drink and she needed food. Her and the bairn. Milk and water was all that had passed their lips in two days.

The drone and the people and the girl in the river was miles back.

She had left the wood behind them and skirted a hamlet crossed a fell and walked without direction. Without thought. The baby's breathing was unsteady now. Dangerously so. The clock of it was ticking now.

The hills took them.

When she stopped to urinate it burned. When she held the bairn to her breast to suckle nothing came. She tried to trick it – deceive it with her tender teat – but the baby was not fooled and it cried and kicked and screamed until it resembled a red cabbage swaddled in rags.

She needed a stream. A puddle or a stagnant sump would do. Anything to drink from. She'd even share a trough with beasts or suck the damp from pond weed if she had a chance. Let it turn her stomach sour; she didn't care.

The fathers have eaten a sour grape and the children's teeth are set on edge.

The gratification of those first mouthfuls would be enough.

Thirst as her tormentor.

Thirst like she had never known. A thirst to turn the world yellow. Make her eyeballs tingle and her throat scream. Lips crack. Teeth itch. Panic.

It was more than a craving now and greater than necessity. This thirst was controlling her. It was a form of torture that infected every dry dusty moment. It was shutting her senses down slowly. Sending warning signals. Telling her she was stupid and irresponsible and not deserving of life. Not deserving of the child.

The girl stopped then lowered herself down on straining knees. Her hand hovered over the till and dry shale. She picked out a pebble. Small and flat like a penny bit. Wiped it on her cuff. Placed it under her tongue. Held it there and swallowed. Got some saliva going. Swallowed hard. Got more spittle going. Sucked the stone. Then walked on.

THE FLIES WERE on the squirrel and if they had laid their eggs then they had not yet hatched. No maggots meant it had only been dead a few hours. It was face down. Splayed as if arranged that way for a display.

She crouched to study it. Its eyes were still there – glassy but intact. There were no signs of disease; the fur and claws looked fine too. She checked its neck for puncture wounds. The signs of the stoat or weasel; signs that it had been a quick kill rather than a slow diseased death. There were no holes.

The flies dispersed as she picked it up by its hind legs. As she did something about it shifted.

Its entire stomach was ripped open and its entrails flopped out. A bizarre miasma of blues and reds and greys. They hung suspended like an absurd string of sausages in a butcher's window. The stench hit her as she flinched and tossed the squirrel aside.

Something had got there first and had a go but whatever it was had abandoned it. Grown bored. Found something better.

She was tumbling down the pecking order now; scavenging from the scavengers. And even then she was too late.

There had to be food. Water. Something. Anything. Anything at all.

THE TWO MEN walked in silence and followed the sun from east to west and when it was at its highest they stopped and drank from a stream and the Poacher picked berries and wild rocket and the Priest ate a little and then they drank more water and carried on. The men no longer strode and the dog no longer strained at his lead but instead walked with its nose to the ground stopping only to paw at a wound behind one of its ears where the flies were feeding on an open sore.

SHE PASSED SHEEP who turned in unison and fixed the girl and the child with their hooded eyes. They stared. Unfazed and blank. The girl stared back. When they determined she was neither a threat nor the farmer with something to offer them they gradually returned to nibbling at the grass.

The girl watched them for a moment as they hungrily clipped the turf with their sharp neat teeth. They drew it in and then blankly ground it in a circular motion then repeated the action again and again. Each animal ate the grass in front of it then occasionally took a step forward to broaden its catchment. Their lives seemed blissfully uncomplicated. Their appetite for the grass was insatiable their movements perfunctory.

Sheep needed to drink too. Didn't they?

There must be water nearby.

There shall be.

There had to be.

And then it appeared before her: a darkening of the chewed grass first – a thin lush ridge on the upper hillside. Ten minutes away. The tiniest of slits barely perceptible to the eye. Five minutes away. Four minutes away. Breathless she became. It was visible now. A foot or so below the surface and bordered with green where the sheep had not eaten. A minute away. Water. She could hear it. Seconds away.

She flopped down to it. A puppet with her strings cut. The first gulps were guilty ones; let the bairn suffer for a few more seconds. It slid down her throat like stony silk. Ice cold even in summer. She slurped at it and the more she drank the greater her thirst grew.

Cold water to a weary soul is good news from a distant land.

Nature provides.

She untied the baby and made it drink from the can. Then she drank some more and washed her face. She drank until her belly was a barrel and then she belched and made the baby take more.

It was a satisfaction of sorts. The world was not quite so yellow and the baby was breathing evenly now. Yet still she was starving.

Nature's cruel humour: the stream led somewhere. She followed it down hill and watched it widen foot by foot and within minutes the girl carefully climbed a small crag and turned a corner and there below lay more water than she could drink in ten thousand life times. Another lake.

This one was much smaller than the last. The gentle sloping at either side suggested it was shallow; it was too small to host a steam boat and its shores too inaccessible to welcome the walkers in their droves. It sat like a puddle in the bottom of a shorter valley. A low wooded hill at one end and a short gravel shore at the other.

Further along the water beyond the wood was a cluster of houses. Houses hold people and people possess food. The day was dwindling. She headed towards the low buildings.

The baby mewled all the way. Its cries drifted out across the water. She walked quickly with her head down and chest heaving. Perspiring. Nearly spent.

The white dead skin of the first burst blister had long rubbed itself away to reveal a raw sovereign of red flesh on her heel and with each step a stabbing now shot through her foot so strong that the girl felt it in her teeth. She was hobbling badly. The baby was crying and gasping and its breaths were becoming laboured and uneven again. Its mouth a wet circle of anguish. The trees grew taller or perhaps it was she who was diminishing.

THE RED ONES with the white dots she knew were poisonous. They advertised their dangerous potential quite clearly; that was how they flourished. You didn't need to be told to know. Even the slugs stayed away.

Nature's warning signs.

But the small sand-coloured ones. They were OK. They were good. They were right.

She was almost certain of that.

Hadn't they eaten them at St Mary's as a treat in season – poached in milk and served on a heel of bread? Yes. One of the Sisters had picked them herself along with kale sorrel spinach wild garlic and great plate sized slabs of fungus broken from tree trunks. Those the Sisters kept for from themselves to flour and fry in butter. The girls got the smaller forage. It had been late summer or maybe the earliest days of autumn. Then she remembered. When it was warm. When it was wet. When the air was soon to be turning smoky.

This time of year? Perhaps.

She couldn't remember. Her thoughts no longer sat in a line like stepping stones over a stream but instead were scattered far and wide and without formation like buttercups in long grass. Alone and disconnected from their nearest neighbours.

The mushrooms were growing in clusters in the damp moss and decomposing leaves in the shade. Their stalks were so thin they looked barely strong enough to support the elongated umbrella heads that reminded the girl of her dry nipples.

She examined them. Plucked one and sniffed it. It smelt of the soil and little else. She bit the head. Watery flesh. Her body did not stiffen or react to repel or offer warning signs as it did when she had tried other non-edible foraged foods.

Nature's way. She picked and ate another then gave the baby the teat. The mushrooms could wait a moment. The bairn could not.

It squeezed and tugged until her entire breast felt aflame so she pulled the child off it and massaged the nipple herself. She squeezed and pulled at it like it was the udder of the Shorthorn until a trickle of something yellow that looked like blister pus came out the end and then she put the baby back on to suckle and slurp.

It sucked until long after she had gone dry again. Then she undressed it and checked for dirt stains but there was nothing. Like her the child's body was no longer producing.

Afterwards it screwed inwards again and stayed that way; its mouth a dry inverted hole and its eyes little more than anguished creases in its pale face. It gave the appearance of one who had been dipped in vinegar. When the girl gently shook it its distended tongue protruded lizard-like and then retracted again though its eyes stayed clamped shut and its breath remained a short rasp. She pressed her lips to its forehead and smelled the fine down on the child's head. She breathed it in.

They were in a delph of sorts an overgrown rock-lined basin marked with the scars of spent dynamite charges; an auditorium blasted into the slope of the woods.

Cloudy pools of water gathered at the base of the depression and around it grew weeds and wild grasses and more aggressive ragwort and balsam whose hollow stalks were as thick as the girl's wrist.

Through the thick hanging ropes of ivy the sheer cross-section of the miocene rock was layered like the pages of a closed book.

She pushed a way through the weeds to higher ground. To a wide flat ledge. The trees sat below her and around her.

Laid across her palm the mushrooms were the height of her fingers. They were fragile looking things and already changing in colour from oatmeal to taupe as they began to dry and shrink and shrivel.

She looked at them. Considered them. She needed something. Anything that produced energy. She was exhausted; near spent. There weren't enough to do much damage. Vomiting at worst. There was nothing inside her to lose anyway. She could take the risk.

And God said let the earth bring forth grass and the herb yielding seed and the fruit tree yielding fruit after his kind whose seed is in itself upon the earth: and it was so.

She would try them and wait a while and if they were good she'd mash some up for the bairn and then pick some more for her pocket tomorrow.

Then hunger overtook reason and she found herself scarfing the handful and chewing them quickly. They tasted of the woods – fusty – the taste of dampness and mould and the moist Lakeland earth. Then they turned string-like and stuck in her teeth. She picked them out with a blackened thumbnail.

The mushrooms sat in her stomach; part-chewed and leathery. But she craved more straight away. They seemed fine. The child could eat some later.

She drank some water then scoured the carpet of the wood while she looked for somewhere to sleep for the night.

The birds were roosting. All around the girl they were ruffling and preening and rearranging themselves in the amphitheatre of branches that surrounded this neglected cavity. Their chatter mapped a complex pattern of communication and the differing sounds of breeds interwove their own shrill languages with one another.

She played with the baby a while but it was inactive and disengaged. It stared at her with heavy lidded eyes and when she waved and wiggled a finger in front of it the eyes just kept on staring.

The girl leaned back against the rock and let the last of the sun's rays move over her and through her.

Tomorrow will worry about itself. Each day has enough trouble of its own.

The warmth of the child's mouth spread through her when it sucked her dry nipple and the twilight lullaby of the birds seemed to be sung especially for her. For them; the two of them. Her and the child both. The baby seemed calm. Its blankets were grubby its face streaked with dirt and mucus had formed more flaky frosting around its nostrils but none of that mattered any more. What mattered was the music that the woodland was making and the warmth that spread through her breast and into her chest to fill her with a golden glow. She was free. They both were. There was hope yet.

Because the birds were with the girl. With the both of them. Her and the child. They were on their side. She was sure of it. If they could survive then she could survive. The worms were with her too. And the trees and the clouds. Everything. Together they would guide the way.

She picked up a handful of soil and held it. Rubbed it with her palm. Inhaled it. Breathed it deep. She tasted the forest with her nostrils. Smelled it with her mouth. Touched it with her eyes.

The warmth in her made her consider the setting sun and the sun made her think of fire and fire reminded her of the matches she still carried in her pocket.

Still clutching the baby the girl began to gather wood. She looked down and saw that her breast plate was layered in a soft tawny brown down and the child's face was buried in it. She touched the not yet fully formed feathers with her hand to follow the downstroke and smooth the barbs of this delicate filigree of fibres.

The child blinked up at her. The girl blinked back and this time she felt like a line of communication was open again. They were speaking with their eyes – she was sure of it. The child was communicating love and gratitude to her. It was recognising her as its protector. Its true mother. She was doing the right thing it seemed to say. Yes. She was acting correctly. Godly.

The girl breathed in deeply and felt her lungs slowly fill. Two balloons inside her. They kept expanding. Her chest and shoulders opened up and the scent of the woods made her synapses pop and tingle.

She wondered why she was standing so went to sit down.

The last shafts of the sun were radiating with an increased intensity now. She felt it on her face and in her feathers. She thought of fire again then remembered the matches again and she stood once again.

There was dead wood everywhere. Brittle branches for kindling. She quickly gathered a pile and placed it on the ledge. The birds were still singing. They were approaching a final flourish for the day but cutting through the chorus was the warm thrum of a wood pigeon somewhere uphill.

She considered the tangle of branches gathered before her and the shapes the sunlight created in shadows behind it.

Another wave of warmth washed over and she put the child down then turned away and violently vomited a watery brown slop. It splattered onto the ground – the taste of earth rejoining the earth.

The girl wiped her mouth and then lay back to bask in the sun. She listened to the wood pigeon's call. It was even and comforting. The sound of summer. The sun on her face. Scintillation.

She opened her eyes and remembered the fire again and searched for the matches again. Looked at the woodpile. Closed her eyes. Basked in the sun. Listened to the wood pigeon. Scintillation.

Thoughts seem to skirt her peripheries but by the time they were close to becoming tangible entities or linear considerations they were already drifting away. Forever just out of reach.

The present moment was a jigsaw. The girl saw only one piece at a time.

Then she was on her back and the ground was alive with life. Squirming with worms and grubs and larvae.

She clung to the earth. She wanted to be naked and rolling in it. Wanted to burrow in it. Bathe in it. She wanted to crawl through the soil and consume it – to join the other creatures and be part of the process and do what the noble worm does and enrich and aerate her surroundings. She wanted to hold the soil up and squeeze the juice from it – to taste the life rub it through her hair through her downy feathers. Wanted to be buried head first in it with only her feet protruding.

The girl understood that the world was round and she was clinging to the side of it. Everyone was. Even the Sisters believed that now.

She listening to the rustle of life around her again. The burrowing and the scratching and the skittering and the scuttling. She heard the slow groan of the tree roots beneath. Heard the unfurling of a balled-up beetle. The reedy click of a hatching moth's wings. The rasp and sigh of something unseen. She sighed and contributed her own noise. Became a part of it.

She turned her head to one side and wished she was not alone; wished she could share this. The ground reciprocated by bending to the girl in a conversation of whispers. Each weed and leaf and blade moved to accommodate her. The insects came to greet her. The spiders and ants rustled through their jungle to bask in the light that was bursting out of her. All creatures in the woods and on the fells above were turning to her. Bewitched and entranced. The rabbit and the hare. The fox and the badger. The squirrel and the vole. The stoat and the mouse and the rat and the weasel. All of them. From their burrows and branches and sets and holes they turned to her and the golden child. Burning in the night. Two creatures on fire.

For the wolf shall dwell with the lamb and the leopard shall lie down with the young goat and the calf and the lion and the fattened calf together; and a little child shall lead them.

The child.

She turned to it and saw a soft crown of light around the baby and she saw its edges blur. The baby was vibrating. The baby was golden too. The sunlight spread through the girl; honey filled her veins and tiny bubbles popped and fizzed at the base of her neck.

She pressed a hand to the child and stroked its cheek.

The girl looked at it with love then watched as coarse black hairs sprouted across its face. The hair grew as if at high speed. It reminded her of the breeze across the lake's surface or how she imagined the sea to be when she reached it.

The child was part of this too. The child was a creature. Part of the landscape. Part of the continuation of growth. The cycle of life.

Soon they would see that sea. She wondered what it would smell of and what it would taste like. And would it be bigger than Lake Windermere?

First they would rest up in a faraway town so big that they could slip down the side streets and back alleys unnoticed and there would be food to forage in abundance and then when they were rested and fed they would walk the rest of the way to the water. Then they would cross it. Somehow they would cross it. She felt sure that this was possible now. All they had to do was get through the mountains first.

Or perhaps the water would part for them. Probably this would happen. The test would be to get to the sea and then He would do the rest. *Lift up your staff and stretch out your hand over the sea and divide it that the people of Israel may go through the sea on dry ground.*

There they would walk on until they found an island and they would make it theirs. And so the waters would close behind them.

The thought of the child growing up in her care was less of an abstract concept now.

She saw a bold and beautiful young lady who would look after her in later life and maybe the child would grow into a woman who was strong enough and clever enough and beautiful enough to pick a man with which to start a new civilisation. With God's will *she* would choose one and *they* would do as she told them. And in the future everything would be different.

The matches were still in the girl's hand. She turned the box over. There was a picture in miniature on the front. A delicate drawing of couples dancing in an opulent ballroom. Elegant women in billowing dresses of varying colours were being lifted and swept across the floor with grace by men in top hats and tails. Their noses cocked into the air. The men had moustaches and the women had clear white skin. In the background was a band – a string quartet – and above them hung a cut-glass chandelier. Everyone looked clean and confident. Their faces flushed. She saw all this because the girl was there with them. She was in the scene sitting off to one side. She could hear the music she could hear the chatter she could hear the squeak of expensive leather.

Then one of the men was gliding across the polished wooden floor that had been laid in a pattern that seemed to repeat itself into infinity. The man's hair was oiled and styled. His hair was so black it was blue. He was very handsome. She could smell him; his scent was exotic.

Then he was before her and he was smiling and bowing and offering a hand. His fingernails were manicured and buffed. They appeared silver in the light. The girl gave him her hand. She made to rise from her seat but could not move. Her body was weighted down. Her body was made of stone. She tried with all her force to rouse herself but nothing happened.

The man dropped her hand. He turned and departed and disappeared into the swirling crowd of waltzing bodies.

The girl turned her head to one side to look across the room and as she did she left the ballroom she left the matchbox she saw nothing but trees and dirt and a pile of sticks; a child and the setting sun and a sour sadness in her empty stomach. But she could still hear the music of the string quartet and the squeak of new leather on the polished floor.

Her hands shook as she removed a match from the box and slowly ran the pink tip along the coarse lighting strip. Nothing happened. She did it again. Still nothing. Again. Nothing.

Again.

Nothing. Again.

Nothing.

She pressed harder and then the match finally took as its head ignited in a small explosion. The phosphorescent smell strong and familiar. Sparks danced within the flame and then it formed into a definite shape with corners and became a radiant octagon that was adjoined on all sides by other octagons some of them the colour of the trees and others the colour of sky. She trailed the flame and saw the octagons shift and jostle until a fragile honeycomb aligned itself across the girl's vision. The match burned for hours. She watched the stick dwindle between her fingers to carbonise black and crooked and then the flame was burning her fingers and then it was out.

She delved into the infinite honeycomb and found another match. Struck it. Nothing. Again. Nothing. Again. Explosion. Fire. The swaying of the flame.

She touched it to the kindling and watch the flame grow. The kindling took. The girl stared at it. She heard the groan and crackle of the wood. The hiss and spit deafening.

The fire had sharp edges. It was a solid thing. All angles and blades. And at its core: pure whiteness. So pure it brought her to the brink of tears.

The bark on the logs peeled back and blackened in the flames. The smoke billowed and floated away in tiny grey cubes. The girl looked at the child and it was no longer covered in hair. She stood and stretched. She sat against the rock and closed her eyes and when she opened them the sky was dark and the trees had turned into massive upended knives and the burning logs were screaming in pain and the fire was a diabolical over-sized bird that was too large for flight. It was spitting and writhing in its white ashen pit.

It was screaming.

It was evil.

ALL NIGHT LONG the forest was made of black glass and it held the girl prisoner. If she moved the glass would crack. If she stood it would lacerate her feet. Everything was as dark as pitch and beyond the giant glass shards and columns there were people. The people were out there. They had broken hands and when they moved they were silent and they wanted the child. They were put on this earth to find it. They wanted to hack the child to pieces. They needed its blood to live in the forest of glass and if she even dared to breathe they would hear her. She was sure of this. If she moved they would hear her. Because they could hear everything. Because they were out there stalking the shadows. These glass creatures of the black black night. They would slit the child's throat and drink the viscous liquid straight from the pumping vein. And they would watch as the black blood fell on black glass. Ran down it. Dripping to the glass floor.

Their lips sanguine the glass black. The night eternal. The fire dead.

10.

THEY FOLLOWED THE basin's rim then after a few minutes they entered it. They clambered over rocks and mud. The dog first. Then the Poacher. Then the Priest.

That stuff you keep putting up your nose Father. What is that – snuff?

No.

Is that why you hardly sleep asked the Poacher. Because of that stuff?

There are more important things than sleeping right now.

Is that so.

Yes.

Like what?

Like thinking. Planning. Praying.

You know what I pray for Father?

The Priest did not respond.

I said you know what I pray for Father? Stewed steak. I pray for stewed steak done the proper way – slowly and with plenty of onions and carrots in there too. I bet Persey would like a taste too wouldn't you boy? And do you know what I'd have to go with it? A nice jug of Alan Gunnerside's foaming ale. Have you tried it Father?

What now.

I said have you tried Alan Gunnerside's foaming ale?

I'm praying.

What – while we're walking?

Yes. While we're walking.

Praying for what.

They worked their way down to the floor of the old overgrown hollow.

That you'll shut up for once.

That's funny that Father.

It wasn't meant to be.

What are you really praying for?

Again the Priest did not respond.

I said what are you really praying for?

A sign.

A sign?

Yes.

What type of sign?

Anything that points us towards the girl.

Like a burned out fire and a heap of shredded mushrooms Father?

They stopped and before them the dog was sniffing around a blackened patch of earth and making excitable whining sounds. The Poacher let it run free and it ran over to a nearby tree and licked at the ground. Then it urinated on it.

The Poacher whistled it back and scratched behind his ears.

Good boy he said. Looks like He is speaking to us after all Father.

THE HOUSE STOOD alone. Its frontage was a blank-eyed mask without a face to wear it.

An adjoining barn stood derelict. Forlorn and spectral. Its windows smashed. There was a large doorway without a door that looked like a gaping mouth after a tooth extraction.

The girl approached it at dawn through the long wet grass.

She could not stay down there in that quarry. The trees had turned on her and joined her pursuers; she had to keep moving. The wood had done something to her. Toyed with her. Turned her brief tranquillity into a fear like she had never known. The poisonous mushrooms had contorted her senses. Sent her head west. Only the flicker of that flame had kept her centred in the night and reminded her of where she was. Helped stave off the enemies. Saved her and the child. Protection by fire just as it always had been.

She went first to the barn and looked in through the glassless window. Saw rubble fallen beams old rags broken glass weeds sheep droppings crockery a shoe. A ladder that led to a hay-loft. Its flat boards were rotten and the stale smell of mildew and abandonment hung heavy.

She moved along to the house and cupped her hands to her brow and saw the living room. There was a fireplace with a huge lintel above it. The hearth was ashen and unswept and the carpet worn and faded from fifty years of life but no sunlight. An upright piano stood in the corner; it was deflated-looking and dusty and looked as if it had never known music.

The next room. An old parlour last used as a bedroom. A steel-frame spring-based bed with no mattress. Book case with books. More on the floor – splayed and scattered. Damp pages dried aloft. A wardrobe with one door hanging open; empty except for dust and coat hangers.

Out front built into the steep hillside there was a small walled-off overgrown garden incongruous amongst the vast space of the fell that surrounded it. It was a tiny once-tamed square of growth on the sloping ground just big enough to grow a few rows of vegetables.

Beside it a rotten potting shed was completely overtaken by weeds and beside it hung a washing line with the pegs still attached.

Creepers and cracks. Lichen and rubble.

It was just starting to get light. Mist sat in the lower part of the valley. The hallucinations had finally abated.

She had not slept.

The girl walked around the back to where the house was cut into the hill where there had been just enough room to fit a wood store and a coal bunker before the hill sloped steeply upwards. There was no wood. There was no coal. Only cobwebs.

She tried the back door. Locked. She jimmied the back window and some of the frame came away in wet splinters. She pulled it again and it opened.

Forgive us our trespasses.

The girl removed the child from her back and put it down in the empty wood store then climbed through the window and into the kitchen sink. She crouched for a full minute. The space was stale – silent – and without habitation so she unlatched the back door then retrieved the child and walked back into the house.

She checked the cupboards and the pantry. There was nothing but soap powder a tea towel a bag of mouldy flour and a large jar of something she couldn't identify. Round objects. Like little brains.

She opened the jar and inhaled the tingling sting of vinegar. She rolled her sleeve up and plunged her arm in up to the elbow and pulled out one of the pickled objects. It was hard. Rock-like. She sniffed it she licked it she tentatively bit into it. It gave. It was wood-like. A walnut. She put the rest into her mouth and chewed. It softened. Tasted good. Then she ate a another.

No water came from the tap at the kitchen sink. She poured the vinegar away and then took the rest of the walnuts and wrapped them in the dirty tea towel. One she kept aside and crushed with the ball of her hand into tiny fragments for the child.

There were stone steps leading down to a cellar. She ducked her head and followed them into a cold store beneath the house. It had a dirt floor and bow ceiling. Stone shelves.

There was another jar. She reached for it and unscrewed the lid. More pickled items. Small cucumbers this time. She pulled one out and sniffed it then bit into it with a crunch. It was sharp. She winced then ate many more.

A wooden packing crate sat in the corner. She rifled through mouldy rags and bits of wire; through fishing line and twine and string. There was a cardboard box containing assorted tacks and nails. A spirit level and a notebook.

Her fingers fell upon a large wrench. She moved it out of the way and saw what looked like a bird's nest. Something moved in it. Her hand retracted and she heard a rustle. She stepped backwards.

She moved back to the crate and dug deep again to part the rags and there in the nest were half a dozen tiny pink hairless creatures curled into half circles. Blind and squeaking their pinhole eyes were still covered by membranes. Their skin was translucent and their organs purple-blue and visible beneath it. Faces barely formed. Baby rats. Only miniscule claws and rounded snouts that sniffed at the air hinted at the creatures they would soon become.

She moved the rags back over them and then took a spool of the fishing line and put it in her pocket.

In the front room the girl stood at the piano and placed her fingers on keys stained yellow by years of nicotine. She pressed down and the piano gave a discordant shriek. The sound of revelation. It seemed to fill the entire house. Animate it. It scared her. Made her aware that she was in someone else's home. Made her feel like they could return at any moment.

The carpet runners on the stairs were made from brass. She touched one. Ran a finger along it. The stairs creaked as she climbed them. The well was narrow. They were steep. There was no hand-rail.

There were rooms on either side of the landing. One with a fireplace and one without. Both were devoid of furniture. There was little worth salvaging – nothing of use but the house itself and even that felt haunted by someone else's memories now polluted by her intrusion.

Then out of the corner of her eye she saw a movement.

The girl froze at the sight of herself in an ornate mirror that was dirty with squashed insect spots and ancient denture spittle.

A wild wide-eyed replica stared back; dirt-streaked and fearful. She moved closer to the mirror and studied a face she barely recognised.

Mirrors were not allowed at Mary's. Mirrors were vain and sinful. Mirrors were made by the devil.

The creature was made subject to vanity – not willingly – but by reason of him who hath subjected the same in hope.

But shop windows and still ponds and the curves of copper kettles could not be avoided so she saw her face on occasion – of course she did: lumpen and mealy-mouthed. A crooked nose too big for her face. Her hair always at all angles no matter how many brushstrokes and lice combs she ran through it.

She saw her strong shoulders and the rise of her chest and a freckle or too that she hadn't noticed before now brought to the surface by this long summer's sun.

Turn my eyes from looking at worthless things; and give me life in your ways.

Voices. There were voices. She heard their low timbre followed by laughter. She dropped to her haunches out of sight.

It was light now. The morning sun was shining into the room. The house had been built to maximise the limited light. It warmed the worn carpet and her movements stirred up dust from it. Each particle turned and swirled then fell.

She raised her nose to the stone sill of the mullion windows. Three men were passing by not more than twenty yards away in the field out the front. Three men in the early hours. Lurking laughing smoking.

Hunters. Woodsmen.

Night lurkers.

They wore long coats. They had their hats pulled low and cigarettes jammed between their lips. They talked without touching them. They had come from the woods and two had rifles slung casually over their shoulders. The other wore something elaborate around his neck. The girl looked and saw that it was an over-sized necklace of dead animals strung to a line. She couldn't tell what. Together they looked like a mythical entity; a horrific hybrid of teeth and claws and black and tan fur. Dead eyes. Devilish and no two ways about it.

They were nearly at the house now. One of them turned and looked uphill – looked at the house.

The girl ducked down again and prayed the child would not make a sound.

She heard their words pass by – coarse and clipped and let loose from beneath fat tongues – weighed down by dialect. A minute passed before she rose. The men were gone and now carving a trail through the long wet grass; their carrion already a target for the bluebottles that trailed them and a languid cloud of blue cigarette smoke lingering above the field like the silk gossamer strands of kiting spiders.

WITH EACH HOUR the child was changing. For the first time the girl was aware of the bones that created its face. It was ageing way beyond its months and its skin reminded her of that of the infant rats; translucent and tight across its delicate inner workings.

Its dark eyes appeared sunken in its face now and its skull more bulbous. The head was too big for the body and the bones of its nose and brow formed a T-shape where once there had been soft flesh. The child's lips were dry. A tongue hung from its circular mouth. What little hair it had was thin and dirty.

Crying required excess energy and it had so little that it remained silent for long periods. Its breathing was short and bordered on the frantic.

The girl walked all day. Followed the sun. Resolved never to stop so long as her legs carried her.

Blisters racked the balls and heels of her feet and the toes of her left foot kept curling and cramping. She walked slowly now. Her strides were automatic and the child grew heavier on her back .

The weather held though and that helped.

She ate the walnuts and she ate the pickles and she crushed them and she fed them to the child and when they rested she was able to expel a feeble amount of watery milk.

She was hungry all the time. Food was all she could think about. She chewed blades of grass to keep her mouth busy and drank lots of stream water to fool her stomach. She felt frail from the mushrooms. Fragile. She had the sensation of being watched wherever she went.

She thought about the house and the noise the piano had made. The nest of rats. She thought about the presence of other people still there in the worn patch of carpet that had led from front door to kitchen. That feeling that life had happened there once – people had been born there and people had died there.

And then she knew why the house had been familiar to her: it had unearthed another deeply-buried memory. That of the old life. Those earliest years as part of a family.

She remembered shapes in a room and feelings of confusion. Parents and siblings who were nothing but faceless forms. Malevolent bodies. Even now she wasn't sure what was memory and what was myth.

She remembered how the leg of the kitchen table had looked and she remembered the stone floor and she remembered being close up to the sky on those moors. She remembered feeling trapped in a room. Remembered a barn. Remembered a cat – maybe. After that only the orphanage. The workhouse. The church. Whatever it was.

Father's favourite they called her. And every time she was sent for the Sisters got angry because it was she and not they who he invited to his praise-giving seminars. And when she returned to the dorm her sheets were wet with ice water or her pillow stuffed with holly and hawthorns or a handbell was rung at her bed-side or breakfast was over and dinner sent to the stray dogs of the town and supper brought a beating.

WHEN SHE LOOKED at the baby the girl reimagined it in a better future decades down the line. A new version. She saw the pair of them together and the child had grown into an individual – a beautiful creature of good physique and intellect and who was generous and compassionate too and the child – now an adult – would feed her clothe her scrub her back in the bath and comb her hair. They would have a house and a garden with a stream running close by because the sound of running water is good for the spirit.

Other times she looked down at the child and saw it for what it was: a tiny helpless creature with a slowing heart-rate and an over-sized skull and an old man's eyes and a desperate inverted mouth and translucent white skin and a rib cage so delicate it didn't look real. And in those moments the very worst thoughts passed through the girl's mind – thoughts of sharp rocks and deep ravines and ropes and rapids and fire and burial; thoughts of a mercy killing – of sobbing as her bare hands clawed at the earth and snot ran from her nostrils and when this happened she would bite her forearm. She would just sink her teeth right in until pain screamed through her and she was jolted out of this horrific thought process that felt less like the dark workings of her imagination and more like a premonition or a compulsion as if a greater force was guiding her propelling her forcing her to commit the great inevitable. The ultimate sin.

WALKING AWAY FROM the main tracks and lanes was exhausting. The ground was uneven and the girl constantly found herself reaching dead ends; impassable bramble patches and sulphur bogs and deep cracks in the earth. Ravines half full of rock falls and fast-flowing streams too wide to cross. Open spaces made her vulnerable while closed-in places like the rutted old cart trail dug into the hillsides made her think of ambushes. She fought against the terrain as best she could. Her ankles ached and the sores on her feet screamed. She found herself periodically gripped by a tremble that she could not shake off. The walnuts and pickles made her stomach ache. Everything ached. The damp dawns made her aware of her bones inside her like a rusted framework.

That night she used the fishing wire to set snares.

She looped them and pegged them along a fence at the bottom of a fell where rabbit runs were clearly visible and where she found burrows and a smattering of droppings.

The fell plunged down into another disused quarry that had come alive with rabbits when she had stumbled while crossing it that evening. A dozen had scattered in all directions: some into gaps between rocks and boulders and others up the gravel bank and away into the meadow above where their tunnels lay.

Pieces of old machinery littered the quarry. Rusted gnarly forms made of wheels and spikes and barrels and corkscrews and giant cogs and mangled chains. Their parts solidified by neglect and rain. Mining detritus; remnants of the old ways.

She set the snares. Twenty of them or more until her fingertips were sore and the light was nearly gone and then she walked out of the quarry and higher up the fell. She could think of little more than the sound of animal fat dripping onto a bed of roasted logs and soft flesh filling her mouth.

Whoever is slothful will not roast his game but the diligent man will get precious wealth.

The girl sat down beneath the buttress of a crag and held the child tight.

She bared a breast and the child took it but no colostrum came. She let it suck until she was sore in the hope that the illusion of milk would be sustenance enough. It wasn't. She found her dolly rag and re-tied it again so that it looked like a human form once more and waved it in front of the child's face.

Then they slept fitfully with the child's breath slow against her ear and the foul scent of it strong.

YOU WILL PAY.

The Priest was murmuring in his sleep. First he had slept lightly then he had dreamed of the girl beyond the hunter's reach and now his words were a slur trailing from a dry mouth.

You will pay for that.

His mutterings woke the Poacher whose fingers instinctively reached in his coat for his knife as he turned over and saw the Priest on his back with his hands crossed on his chest. Like a corpse he thought. Even in sleep he does not let his guard down.

The Poacher could just make out his profile: the arch of his nose the elongated upper lip and the crude slit of a mouth. His fine red hair swept backwards.

His legs together. Boots pointed skywards.

The Priest was babbling. Speaking in tongues.

Then his face was screwed up and frowning as he started scratching furiously as if at an invisible coffin lid; his hands a blur in front of him as if he were being buried alive.

His whole body was thrashing now. Tossing and turning in the dirt and leaves.

And all the while the Priest was making these strange noises. Hissing and moaning sounds. And between the noises the Poacher heard snatches of phrases that unnerved him and made him sit up. Made him see the Priest in a new light.

Ungrateful sinful fucking whore treacherous imbecile bitch daughter of Satan he hissed.

Father said the Poacher.

Dirty unwashed bastard spawn of stinking peat bog inbred fucks.

His hands had stopped thrashing now. Hearing the men the dog awoke and stood and strained on its tether. Its teeth bared it strained towards the Priest.

You filthy scabby....yes. Get down on your knees and thank the lord Jesus for this gift you are about to receive.

Father. You're having a nightmare.

The Priest's head rocked from side to side. He moaned low and throaty.

Drink it down and may you be truly grateful. That's it. That's it. Forgive all trespassers. Oh Father oh God oh for the bloody body of Christ and the screaming soul of Mary Magdalene.

The Poacher threw back his blanket and shouted.

Father.

The dog gave a low gurgle then a snarl.

The Priest opened his eyes his hands crossed his chest once again. He turned his head.

Fucksake Father. You were talking.

The Priest looked at him.

Go back to sleep he said quietly and with a calmness that the Poacher found unnerving.

Still standing Perses looked from the Priest to the Poacher then back again.

How can I with you blethering and thrashing like a wraith.

What did I say?

Nothing said the Poacher. You said nothing.

You said I was talking.

The Poacher scratched the end of his nose.

You were talking nonsense. Weird noises. Nightmare stuff.

Are you sure. Nothing intelligible?

What's intelligible?

Nothing you could make out.

Nothing I could repeat Father. No.

Then go back to sleep.

The Priest turned his back and the dog settled down again with its chin on its paws.

The Poacher was sitting up on one elbow.

It'll be light soon he said. The Priest grunted.

Yes.

They fell silent for a moment under their thin blankets. In the leaves.

Father.

What.

It sounded like you were having quite a dream there.

It's a habit I have sometimes. Mumbling in my sleep.

Right. Mumbling Father.

When I'm overworked.

Is that so.

Yes.

I've never been much of a nightmare man myself said the Poacher. I've always been a heavy sleeper. They say it's all the fresh air and exercise. Mind – I do most of my sleeping in the day-time. Night-time in the woods is a day in the office for me.

I didn't say I was having a nightmare said the Priest. You said that. Not me.

Sounded pretty strong from here Father. Vivid like. Detailed.

Why – what did I say?

The Poacher smiled to himself in the darkness.

Nothing Father. Nothing. Go back to sleep. And sweet dreams.

SCREAMS FOLLOWED SCREAMS. A distant cawing out there – the curdling sounds of animals that lasted all night. Soon they began to sound like tortured children. Like creatures facing death. The girl had to put her fingers in her ears and curl herself into a ball to avoid a confrontation with her past. If she let them win her bones would turn to dust.

HOURS PASSED WITHOUT a word being exchanged.

The day was bright and warm now and it hummed with swathes of insects that were swarming above the meadow when they saw the abandoned house.

They walked through waist high grass towards it. The dog. The Priest. Then the Poacher.

As they neared it the dog became re-energised and charged into the outbuilding but came straight back out again and ran to the rear of the house and through the open back door.

Look at him said the Poacher.

She's been here said the Priest.

The dog went into each room in turn and ran in a circle then moved to the next one. It whined with excitement then climbed the stairs in three leaps.

Right said the Poacher. Time to find me some grub.

He searched the kitchen cupboards and when he couldn't find anything he kicked a door right off its hinges then went into the cellar and began to ransack it.

The Priest went upstairs and looked in each room then stood at the window. He leaned on the stone mantel with both hands and bowed his head. He breathed deeply.

She had been there. He could feel it. Her presence. Life had recently been in this dead dust-settled room.

He closed his eyes and whispered to himself:

As the deer pants for streams of water so my soul pants for you O God.

He reached for his vial.

AT DAWN THE baby kicked out and it woke her. Shivering the girl stood and left the sleeping parcel in the cold shadow of the overhang and walked down to the quarry. She could barely lift her feet. She kept to its edges. Avoided the flat open space.

The first snare she checked was just as she left it – a small looped slipknot invisible to the eye were it not for the twig she had used to peg it. There was no rabbit. The second was the same. And the third.

On she walked dragging her feet – stopping then stooping and her stomach growling. With each empty snare her feet felt heavier. All were as she had left them.

Not a single one had worked.

In famine he shall redeem thee from death.

Holding a rock cupped in one hand she sat on a boulder and watched as rabbits appeared one by one from breaches and crevices as if to taunt her. She didn't move. When one was in range she stood and prayed for intervention then threw the rock. Hurled it with as much force as she could. Hoped that He would feel her hunger and guide her hand. It missed by a long way and landed with a flinty crack that resounded around the dusty quarry. Maybe He wasn't watching. Maybe He had abandoned her.

Maybe He had never been there at all.

The rabbits fled once more. She picked up a smaller pebble and put it in her cheek.

Out of the depths I cry to you O Lord.

THE CHILD'S TINY nostrils flared. The scent of muck-spreading in a lower pasture had stirred it. Each hour brought a new aroma and this sweet scent of excrement made the child salivate. Reminded that it was hungry.

They were resting in a tiny cemetery. The headstones were cracked and angled. The grass untended. No flowers were held in the broken vases that sat in their shadows. There was no church only this fenceless burial ground that was slowly being reclaimed by the grasses and weeds that surrounded it. The baby saw a face looming over it and reached out to grab at grubby cheeks and a greasy nose. The mouth of the face widened into a smile and the child forgot its hunger for a moment and smiled too. Eye to eye. The baby let out a gurgle and then the smile of the girl faded and the smile of the baby faded with it and thick cloud passed overhead blotting out the sun dropping the temperature and drawing a shade across the cemetery. Across the mountain.

THE POACHER STOPPED and dropped to his knees.

Look.

The Priest crouched on his haunches beside him.

There was a rabbit trapped in a snare. Dead eyed and asphyxiated. Pegged by the fence.

The Poacher freed it.

It's still warm. That's fresh is that.

How fresh?

I'd say no more than three hours. Tops. Maybe less.

It could be anybody's.

The Poacher stood. The rabbit in his hand.

Could be but I don't reckon. Look at Persey.

The dog was sniffing the snare and the grass around it with excitement.

That's not the rabbit that's got him going. Normally it'd be in bits be now. He's got their scent. It must be strong.

They're close then.

I'd say so.

How far?

How long's a piece of string Father.

The snare. Could she have made it?

The Poacher looked at the wire then pulled out the peg from the soil. Studied it.

Looks a bit shoddy. Primitive. But it has worked. Whoever's done it has scouted the area. Found a run. Got some knowledge. I'd wager you look around this field and there'll be more of these about. I thought you said this lass of yours was feeble minded?

The Priest said nothing.

There must be something about her for you to be doing all this Father. Days we've been away. Half starved and stinking. All for some stupid lass who's not as stupid as she's letting on.

The Priest turned to the Poacher. They were standing close. So close the Poacher could smell the Priest's breath. Stale. He looked into the Priest's dark eyes. Saw darkness saw receding gums saw the mapped marking of burst capillaries around his nostrils.

I told you. I'm here for the baby.

You said that. But I'm just wondering if maybe there's more to all this than you're letting on. I mean murder –

The Priest's arm shot up as he slapped the Poacher across the cheek with an open hand. The dog growled and then barked.

You're not here to wonder.

The surprise hurt the Poacher more than the blow. His cheek burned the colour of humiliation.

I wouldn't advise doing that again Father. You might find the hound chewing your nose off.

The dog doesn't scare me. And neither do you. I've got a stronger weapon than any you could care to name.

That right.

Yes. It's called faith.

The Priest turned and started walking. The Poacher felt the inside of his cheek with his tongue then spat. There was blood.

So it's true what they say isn't it Father.

The distance between the two men grew and the dog stood in the middle confused and conflicted.

About you and them lasses up at St Mary's the Poacher shouted after him.

The things you do I mean he said. You and them girls.

The nuns just letting it go on he said.

It's all true isn't it he said.

Isn't it Father.

All true.

FROM THIS FAR distance it looked like a stream the way the ribboned strip appeared to run down in the gap between two steep boulder-strewn fells. An ashen spate heavy with dolomite dust. Smoke-coloured and slow-moving.

But as the girl got nearer she saw the surface was too flat and static to be a stream. It held no sheen to it.

It was a road. A new artery laid down where an old cart track had once followed the undulating contours of the land to climb and wind through a series of humpbacks and cut-backs.

The pass had been in use for centuries. From packhorses to charabancs it had been the only way that traders who carried anything more than the goods on their back could get through the mountains to the lake and the towns that lay beyond. The trail lead to the Western fells and the county had invested a lot of money to cover the many cavities and craters that hundreds of years of footfall and wheels and weather and hooves had hammered. Now it had been smoothed out into a long tarmacadam road that fluttered like a kite's tail up into the distance before her.

The pass was only two miles long – three at the very most – but she could see that they were hard miles. In places the road climbed so steep it was hard to imagine even a horse making it through.

The last of the pickled cucumbers were gone and only a few walnuts remained. She would ascend the pass famished. Walking on empty.

The flanking fells were featureless and as green as they would get for the year. They held no bracken for cover though – only sheep-nibbled grass and glacial till. From down below they appeared to run right on up to the sky like stairways.

The terrain up there was too rough and untrodden. Too exposed. Unless she turned back the pass remained the only the way through to wherever it was she was going. Forwards was her only destination; instinct told her so. To turn back and re-trace her steps now would be suicidal. A move that no other hunted creature would consider.

The girl would have to stick close to the pass but not walk on the road itself. If she could follow its topography while keeping herself hidden as best as she could she and the child might make it through unseen.

The girl leaned into the land and dug in with her toes. She felt her knees strain and her thighs burn. She could smell vomit. She could smell excrement.

The camber made her crooked and her hip hurt. So did the burning coin-shaped circles of raw flesh where once there had been blisters. She felt a tightening of the throat. Bile rising.

THEY SAT APART.

The Poacher pulled something from his coat pocket. Braces of tiny tied birds. Sparrows and tits. A dozen of them. He leaned against a tree and deftly tugged away their feathers then he skewered them and roasted them over a fire.

When what little fat was on them was hissing and dropping onto the glowing remains of the burning logs he slid them off the stick and gnawed at their tiny wings. He stripped them of their flesh and sucked the juice from their fragile bones. The feathers he threw on the fire and the other remains he shared with his dog. Grease coated his lips. He belched.

The Priest sat on a log with his eyes closed and his head full of powder as he muttered silent prayers. Immovable.

THE GIRL ASCENDED the barren chicane. Committed to it.

Staying off-road made it even harder.

The pass was famous; one part of it had long been nicknamed The Struggle by locals. After a while – when the thought of them became insurmountable – she ate the few walnuts that were left. Hunger overtook pragmatism – she didn't even give any to the child. The child didn't need the energy to walk. She did. She needed the sustenance. It was her role to get them through. To take them elsewhere. To a new town maybe – to the land beyond. Whatever lay there. Peace and serenity and silence she hoped. No violence no more starvation. No cold morning showers; no sadistic Sisters. Just her and the child and a belief in a good God. A true God. A real God who wanted to love them and protect them and reward them for their devotion and purity.

The one who endures to the end will be saved.

She would walk to the horizon and then everything would be alright. Yes. She was sure of it. Yes. It had to be. Beyond the horizon was where life began. It would be better there. Yes. It had to be.

Yes.

The road kept rising. Each corner spawned a new curving escalation. The pass was an illusion; an endless Jacob's Ladder.

The walk grew purgatorial as it guided her through a series of teases and false endings like a recurring nightmare about movement without distance. Only when the girl stopped to catch her breath and turned to look back did she know that she was progressing forwards and upwards.

The child remained silent. It unnerved her. She untied the sling and lifted it off her back and its head rolled. Glassy eyes saw right through her. She clicked her fingers by its ear but got no reaction. Its breath could barely be heard. It was nothing more than the sigh of a newborn runt kitten.

... and the breath came into them and they lived ...

The girl tried not to panic and concentrated on the horizon instead. She made the horizon the boundary of heaven and when they got there food and water and warmth would be bountiful and love would await them.

But voices said otherwise. A chorus nagged and mocked her; prodded and cackled and hissed spoke of Father and reminded her of how he said she would always be his and she could never truly leave and if she did he would find her and bring her back for her calling was the Church and she was forever indebted; how she had been sent to do God's work in the community; to be charitable and strengthen the reputation of Mary's through good deeds around the town and besides didn't some of the younger fresher untouched girls need his instruction now? And the way he had turned away from her that last time was worse than the shrieks of the Sisters. Worse than any of their pinches and slaps birches and burns scratches and insertions. Because even though she despised and feared and loathed him his rejection was worse than any of that.

SHE STAYED OFF the pass but followed it closely scrambling hand over foot between boulders. She shrank the universe down to a single footstep and she crossed that universe again and again. It was the only way she could keep moving. She tried to block out the voices and focused instead on the child on her back. The cramp. The blisters. Thirst. Starvation.

She thought of the Bible. She thought of the scriptures. She asked for help and words came in response: *the mountain falls and crumbles away and the rock is removed from its place. The waters wear away the stones; the torrents wash away the soil of the earth; so you destroy the hope of mortals.*

11.

AFTER THEY BUILT him a new sloped roof lean-to round the back the Warden finally cleared out the old wood store. He smoked out a wasp's nest from it and swept the tiny room and then turned it into an office. Now he had a wood burner in there plus a drop-leaf table and a foot locker full of maps and guidebooks and a first aid kit – wire splints gauze compress bandages iodine and iodine applicators; scissors aspirin matches flares brandy the cash box and the log book now tattered and nearly full. Spare oilskins and boots stayed in a shallow built-in wardrobe not more than a foot deep.

The bunkhouse sat just beyond the peak of the pass in a hollow not far off the new road.

There were two rooms: one for the men that had eight bunks built into the pine walls and a table in the middle and one for the women that held four. There was also a small kitchen with a range. The toilet was a hole in a board in a shed out back beside the crag.

The bunkhouse was basic but there was food and warmth and beds and the water was good up there too. Pure and sweet. It came straight through the top sandstone.

His bed was separate from the bunkhouse now and he could eat as much food as he could cook in exchange for running things. He could leave during the day but was instructed to never miss a night.

The Warden's job was to check people in keep the floors clean and the outhouse sterilised. His role was to keep the bunkhouse heated wash blankets and strong arm anyone who got too drunk or unruly or amorous in the night. This had only happened twice before. Once when a fight had broken out between two tarmackers and once when two blond boys from the continent were discovered engaged in a sexual act. Even then he'd stuck one in the wood store and one in the kitchen. Turning people out into the night in such a remote spot was something he tried to avoid. In the winter the exposure could kill anyone within hours. He did not want to shoulder the burden of death.

Three winters ago when it never got above freezing for forty days straight and water came from melting great pots of ice and the pass froze like a waterfall cast in marble the bunkhouse floor was full with shivering bodies under blankets for days. And still he turned no-one away. He rationed the food and kept the burners glowing all hours and welcomed all new shivering arrivals.

It suited him fine. There were new people to meet and many a night the bunkhouse sat empty and he relished the heightened sense of solitude. There was the bird-watching and animal life. There were walks on the tops. Logs to chop and wood to whittle. Dips in the stream. Fixing. Tidying. Cooking. Thinking. Plenty to do.

Once a week the Warden went down to the lake for supplies. The county paid and he always bought extras for the stores. Bunkers were meant to bring their own bait but there were always those who weren't prepared. They'd get lost on a ramble or caught out in the clouds. Lives had been saved because of him. He knew that. Even if was just demonstrating the correct way to lance a blister or read a compass or forcing a slab of parkin on some hapless wanderer setting out with nothing but tobacco in his pocket.

On Wednesdays the county paid a farmer to drop off milk and cheese and eggs on the way to market and oatcakes and cigarettes on the way back that evening. The dairy lasted through to the weekend and on Mondays and Tuesdays he took his tea black.

The most of them were walkers and climbers and he had no trouble with that lot because they were usually students or well-spoken scholars educated in some ways of the world but not in others. Then there were occasional groups there doing land surveys for the government or sent in on reconnaissance missions by the slate mines and lead works. Oftentimes there were farmers too stopping on their way over the tops to markets or country shows over in the Western Fells or up in the Dales. The rest of the bunkhouse population was made up of a variety of herdsmen salesmen itinerant labourers road crews and Romanies.

He didn't get many women though. Even fewer girls. And certainly not by themselves.

AHEAD THE DOG was distracted by something. It had its nose to the ground and was pawing at the earth; pawing at something white in a crevice. A scrap of cloth or paper perhaps.

The Poacher whistled and said Persey but the dog ignored him.

They were walking down a steep bank in a wood. The bank was made of compacted mud with a top layer of decaying leaves. They kept sliding.

The Priest carefully walked over to it. As he reached it the dog growled and shifted sideways flinching. Its back arched. It swiped at its nose. The Priest leaned in and went to pick up the paper.

Dots were streaming out of the white shape in the crevice. Dozens of them. Wasps. The paper was the grey pulp of a nest they had built into this narrow fissure in the ground and which had now been disturbed. The dog fled with a yelp. The wasps went for the Priest. He felt them swirl around his head and tried to swat them but there were too many circling. Some landed. One stung his hand and another his neck. He slipped in the dead wet leaves. A third stung his upper lip. He turned and fled downhill ducking and flapping his hands about his head.

The Poacher had been watching from a safe distance uphill and laughed at this. Seeing the Priest express something other than impatience and disdain was hilarious. The Poacher thought this was the funniest thing he had seen in a long time.

Run Father run he said then laughed harder still.

The leaves gave way and the Priest slipped backwards then slid down the hill grabbing out for roots. For anything.

His coat flapped open and trailed behind him in the dirt and his metal vial bounced around his neck. Panic crossed his face. He slid twenty then thirty feet as his hands clawed at the earth and a trail of wasps followed behind him. The Poacher bent double and laughed long and hard.

The Priest stood and in one fluid movement ran off into the trees. Eventually he stopped. Breathless.

He checked himself for wasps but they were no longer on him. His adrenaline was coursing in reaction to the stings and the fall. His heart thumping.

He turned and looked back up the hill. He could just make out the figure of the Poacher and the dog beside him on the brow of the hill and when he turned to walk away he could still see the Poacher laughing and snorting and slapping his thighs.

IT HAD BEEN two days since the last visitor had left.

The Warden had spent the afternoon sweeping out the bunk rooms and checking the stores and now he was on the porch eating mackerel from the tin while smoking a cigarette and soaking up the last of the evening when a figure peaked the pass. It looked like a witch hunched double. A harridan from the hills like something from an old wood-cut. The figure was slow and unsteady and even from here he could hear it gasping like a death rattle.

He put down his tin and stood. He stepped down from the porch to meet the figure and saw that it was a young lady in as a dire a state as any human he had ever seen. Her face was sweat- and mud-streaked and her skin sallow and bloodless; her eyeballs too big for sockets that appeared to have receded around them. Her clothes were rags and her boots were shapeless clots moulded to her feet. Tangled hair. Blackened hands. Desperate. Like something from the bog he thought. A creature of the soil.

He crossed the hollow that housed the bunkhouse and walked the worn grass down to meet the pass road.

She saw him and stopped. Her torso heaving. And it was then that he saw that the lump on her back was neither a hunch nor a pack but baby-shaped.

Christ lass. Are you alright?

A tongue ran round dry cracked lips but she said nothing.

By yourself are you?

Again silence. A heaving chest. Eyes that barely dared to take him in. When they did finally settle on him she saw a man in a thick blue roll-neck jumper. He wore a beard that masked a younger face beneath.

That's a raw enough climb for anyone said the Warden.

After the silence of the pass his voice seemed loud and booming to the girl – like the after-seconds of a quarryman's dynamite stick.

Rawer still carrying a wean on your back.

Again her tongue ran over dry lips still panting. Her breath chewed between her teeth.

The bairn looks snug but I'd wager you'll both be needing food and a sit down he said.

The girl looked beyond the man to the wood-panelled bunkhouse sitting sturdy against the top slopes.

Doesn't look like you'll have much coin about your person he said. But that's not a concern to me.

The girl's breathing was slowing but her legs stayed planted. Suspicion shrouded her wide eyes.

Tell you what he said with as gentle a smile as he could muster. I'm away to put the kettle on and if you've a mind to you can sit on the porch and rest those feet there. And if that's to your liking there'll be tea mashing and tea cake to go with it and maybe some milk for the bairn. But if it's not and I come back out and you're gone – well – then there's all the more for me.

The girl wiped her mouth with her sleeve.

SHE'LL HAVE GONE up the pass said the Priest. Can't see which other way she'd take.

This was the first thing he had said in some time. He had been sulking. His top lip had come up thick. It was sore to the touch and impeded his speech. This amused the Poacher even more than when the wasps attacked and nearly as much as when the Priest had done the slapstick tumble down the bank.

For the past three hours the Priest had refused to speak to or even acknowledge him. Instead he had unscrewed his vial and snorted more powder to numb the pain of the itching welts that had risen on his thin pale skin. The powder made him walk quicker than ever. The Poacher struggled to keep up. The Priest walked with renewed purpose; with galvanised anger.

Now it was The Poacher who was silent. They sat down across from one another and as the Priest spoke he turned to follow his finger up to where the pass met the clouds.

If we'll do it tonight we'll catch her by the morning. With God's will.

That right Father.

Sooner or later she'll head into a town. She'll have to. I've checked the maps and the pass is the only way through. It's either that or starve up top.

Or someone's taken her in said the Poacher.

No. That's a fool's business. Word will be out by now. There'll be posters up. All eyes will be looking for the lass. We do the pass tonight.

The Poacher lifted his hat then cleared his throat and spat. A green globule stuck to a rock like a land-bound limpet. The dog licked it.

You know I've been thinking Father. When you hired me it was for a straight tracking job. A day or two you said. Help you find this bairn you said – if it exists.

Of course it exists.

That's as maybe. Or maybe not. But either way that time has long passed now Father and unplanned things have occurred and it turns out there's some personal involvement you've not been mentioning either. Now you're a man of God and as you know that's not my interest. That's your lookout. But you're known Father – feared even – and I was prepared to go along with all this. For a bit. But who's to say the same thing won't come of this lass when we catch up with her as did befall old Tom Solomon?

What do you care.

I don't particularly. But she's better than you think this lass. She's no dummy this one. If she was she'd be caught be now. She's got heart. I can tell that. And a head and all. Or the right instinct anyways. Days we've been trailing her and we've not even seen so much as her shadow. Sometimes the hunter can't help but respect the hunted.

Respect scoffed the Priest. You must be out of your narrow backward mind. The girl's stolen a baby man. Someone's child. Does that not matter to you?

Aye – and that's unfortunate. But you're not angelic yourself are you Father. You've been committing your own sins and then dismissing them in the name of God. Them poor lasses. You've been getting right in there haven't you? Course you have. I know what you do Father and I don't like it. Don't like it a bit. You're all at it you religious lot. Beast behaviour. But I'm not a prying man. Secrets are secrets for a reason. So here's what I'm suggesting; you double my payment for services rendered and maybe think about putting the word in for me with that keeper's cottage up on the estate. The gate house. Lovely little place that is and I know you've clout with the councillors Father. I know how the town works. I've got eyes and ears.

The Poacher turned gamekeeper said the Priest. Very good.

Whatever you like Father. You're the word man not me. But you see to it that it's mine from the autumn and I'm liable to keep quiet about all this mess you've made.

And if I don't?

Well I reckon me and Persey will be on our ways.

You think I need you when I'm this close to finding the girl don't you? said the Priest. Well off you go then. You're feckless and useless anyway. Disposable. But the dog stays.

The two men stared at each other for a moment.

Of course not all secrets stay secret shrugged the Poacher. It might be that I stop off at The Shoulder for a drink and a catch-up with the boys on the way. Boys what have daughters of their own. Tough lads but sympathetic in their own ways. Moral like.

You're threatening me said the Priest.

Sex stuff tutted the Poacher. Orphan girls. The church. Bodies in caves. Addictions. Weaknesses. It's not good Father. Not good at all. I mean no institution lasts forever. Things can quickly crumble. Just a few words could cause a dozen cathedrals to fall

The Priest said nothing.

Sleep-talking is a peculiar thing as well said the Poacher. Isn't it Father.

The Priest stood. He faced the Poacher now and then he spoke and when he did his swollen lips peeled back and the Poacher saw that his blue gums were bleeding.

Because he practiced extortion and robbed his brother and did what is not good among his people said the Priest. Behold: he shall die for his iniquity.

Father I'm done with your bible shit said the Poacher.

Ezekiel said the Priest. 18:18.

THE WATER BOILED and the Warden walked to his room and parted the curtains. He looked out. The girl was walking slowly towards the porch. He heard her boots on the creaking timber. She sat.

He went into the main bunk room and crossed it. He reached up and pulled out the tacks that he had used to pin the notice to the wall. It was handwritten and it curled up in his hand. He unfurled it and smoothed it flat. On it it said:

MISSING
HAVE YOU SEEN A GIRL?
WANTED FOR ABDUCTION

16 YEARS OR THEREABOUTS
5FT 6 IN HEIGHT. BROWN HAIR
FEEBLE OF MIND &
BELIEVED TO BE MUTE

NAME OF BULMER

LAST SEEN IN KESWICK
AUGUST 8.

HOLD HER AND TELL THE AUTHORITIES.

He rolled the notice back into a scroll and then went and put it in his foot locker with his other papers and books.

There was no mention of her baby but it was her alright. Had to be.

On the porch the girl had unwrapped the bairn and was holding it up in front of her. Her hands in its armpits. The child flopped limp and loose. He watched from the window. Only the grimace on its dirty face and the slight flexing of one curled hand registered that it was even alive.

He took tea and toasted tea cake and milk out to her.

Special treatment he said. Hope you don't think all guests get this.

The girl wolfed half the tea cake and then drank the tea too quickly and burnt her mouth. He leaned against the rail and faced her.

It's just that you and the bairn look at death's door.

Do not forget to entertain strangers for by so doing some have unwittingly entertained angels.

Ignoring him the girl took another bite of the tea cake; she chewed it and then spat it out into her hand. She formed the paste into a small pellet and pressed it into the bairn's mouth. It fell to the porch floor. A wet mush of bread and saliva. She bent and picked it up and then put it in her mouth and followed it with another large bite of the tea cake.

The Warden's eyes widened.

The bairn was in her lap now. Its eyes were closed. Mouth open. Tongue blue-tinged and distended.

Be dark soon he said trying to keep his voice calm and conversational even though he was unnerved.

She drank more tea and winced at the heat. Didn't even acknowledge him.

No place to be – out there. Even in summer. Up top like.

He gestured towards the fells

Even the pass is pitch and you can't rely on the moon to guide you. Moon has its own ways.

She set her cup aside.

Long way down the other side an all and no telling who's waiting at tuther end.

At this she looked up at him. She looked through him and she looked beyond him. He saw the words were registering with her. He knew he had to be careful.

No-one stays here except on my say so. I've not turned anyone away yet but I could do if they didn't fit right. Troubles are left at the door with the mud from the fells. You'd be safe here.

She looked away from him along the length of the porch.

Wherever it is you're fetching to can no doubt wait another day he continued. There's a bed that's yours. Choice of beds. Hell there's a whole room if you want it. Sun'll be down right enough and then I reckon that'll be us lot for the day.

She wiped her nose.

Got bacon an all he said.

Silence. Then the Warden spoke again.

You can please yourself and I always believe that anyone's business is their business but that baby looks done for he said. If you know what's right you'll do what's right because when all is said and done there's only God to answer to and rightness is all that counts in this life and the next. You'd be best to think on that.

Still looking away the girl nodded. Only just. But there was movement. He saw it. A slight dipping of the chin to the neck.

IT HAPPENED IN the darkest part of the night.

He rose and took a long deep sniff from his vial and the trees looked like rows and rows of crucifixes awaiting bodies. Swaying symbols of a faith in the limitless cathedral.

He walked over to the dog and it growled at him but he patted it a while and got it settled and then he led it away and tied it to a tree then he walked back to the Poacher and unsheathed the Poacher's knife and hacked at his throat. He cut out his voice-box so that he couldn't make a noise as he died there thrashing in the dirt awake but silent with the Priest leering over him with his fine red hair falling forward and his child's teeth grinding together as he slashed and filleted and hacked and tore at the Poacher who was gagging and choking and drowning in himself and the dog was barking and snarling at first then howling then finally silenced when the Priest threw it some fresh meat.

THERE WERE FOOTSTEPS on the bunkhouse porch. The entire building was made of wood. She felt the vibrations.

It was the middle of the night – she could tell from the lack of light through the gap in the curtains – and the bairn was in the bed next to her. More milk and wet crumbs had temporarily roused it though even swallowing had seemed a struggle. Now it was sleeping.

The man who ran the bunk-house had shown kindness but she was anxious and had the fitful shallow sleep of the hunted. The mattress was the softest she had ever experienced. It creaked when she moved and she could not get comfortable. She felt like she was in quicksand; like she was being sucked under.

So she had slept for an hour or so and now her head ached. A sharp stabbing pain ran right up through one side of her neck and deep into her skull ending somewhere behind her left eye. Her jaw ached also. Then the baby stirred and started crying. It had wet itself and wet their bed and now it had wet her too. She sat up and lifted the baby out and put it into the next bed.

There was the sound of coughing and hacking and more shuffling of feet. Boots on wood. Voices of men. She smelled cigarette smoke. Sensed the movement of men.

She desperately needed to urinate but she did not dare leave the room so she squatted in the corner and went as quietly as she could. It trickled across the wooden boards and gathered in a pool in the centre of the room where the floor was sagging. She climbed back into bed and dozed.

IT WAS NOT yet four but already he could hear the first calls of birdsong from down the valley. He watched the glowing logs for a while and shivered in his coat. The sky was cloudless. The sky was endless. The Priest stood and then walked over to the prone body. He crouched.

He reached for the leather bag and he looked inside it. He pulled out some flapjack and broke off a corner and slowly chewed it then he lifted up the hem of the Poacher's trouser leg and saw a dirty woollen sock. He peeled it back and looked and then he laughed. He laughed silently to himself through his mouthful of food.

He took hold of the Poacher's leather boot and he twisted. The foot turned a way. He chewed and swallowed and twisted again harder this time but the foot did not give.

The Priest rolled the trouser leg further up – almost tenderly – and saw that there were leather straps running up to the knee where a band of leather encircled it like a miniature belt. A buckle held it at the back. The Priest took his knife and cut through the leather then he pulled at the boot again. Harder. A jerk. The boot and the wooden foot that was wearing it came away this time. He weighed it in his hand for a moment and it felt heavy. The foot ran halfway up the shin and had a moveable ankle joint. The wood was mottled. He could see the grain of it. In places the varnish was chipped.

The Priest turned away from the body and carefully placed the Poacher's foot on the fire. He prodded at the embers with a stick and watched as the flames took it. The birdsong was getting louder. He watched the glowing foot until it became a shapeless blackened lump.

He said no prayers.

A THIN STRIP of light blue widened in the darkness then disappeared.

The girl was unsure if she had seen it; unsure of whether she was awake or sleeping. She rolled over. Away from the damp patch.

But something in the room had changed. The still air had reconfigured itself into a new shape. There was energy out there – a heartbeat.

Then there was weight upon her. A shape bearing down; a dry hand clamped down on her mouth and a hip bone colliding with her hip bone. Movement. Everything happening at once. She smelled the stench of soil and smoke and sweat – sickeningly strong – familiar yet repulsive and a knee between her legs navigating its way in to unlock her and open her like a bible. She felt the roughness of coarse stubbled hair scratching at her face and neck as if whoever it belonged to was trying to wear her away. Sand her. Erase her. Just scrub her away and file her down to nothing.

Then there was a hand on her then there was a hand up her then there was a hand in her. A foreign body wearing her.

She dared not move. She prayed for the baby in the next bed. She asked Him to end this.

There was no sound but that of breathing; her through her nose and it – he – through his mouth.

There was an adjustment of hips and shoulders – a shifting of the weight – but still the hand was on her mouth gripping her jaw bone clamping her head while the other was in then out then in again. Dry grubby fingers. She tried to close her legs and seal herself off but again the knee came up harder this time slamming into her a bolt of pain jolting right up into her stomach. Pinning her.

Then she was spread and he was in her and he was bigger than the Priest and there was more thrusting and more weight and more everything.

And she didn't know who or what or why this was happening – only that it was and that she had no control and if she just lay still it would not go on forever. The nice man who fed her. He did not smell like this. Did not have that look about him. Did not seem capable. She submitted to whoever. Told herself: this will be the last time ever.

Then darkness and silence followed and the bairn in the next bed had – she thanked God – been left alone and was sleeping.

After everything she thought.

So they are no longer two but one flesh. What therefore God has joined together let not man separate.

After everything – this.

This.

12.

WHEN IT WAS over and the thin line of light had been and gone again the girl stood and there was pain and when she put her hand down there something warm and wet coated her fingers but she did not dare to smell or taste it. Instead she checked the baby. She wrapped it up and then slipping in her own urine in the middle of the room quickly opened the door and moved down the corridor then was off running into the night and chasing the land beyond.

There was a rising burning inside of her as she ran. It moved up through her abdomen and into her stomach and seared up through her chest where it fizzed and gurgled at the back of her throat hot and acidic and she had to stop to heave and spit.

Night surrounded her and the ground was uneven; the bairn a dead weight. A useless parcel. She thought she heard movements the stumbling of shapes and a snorting sound behind her – a clearing of phlegm in the throat – so she turned and ran faster and let the ground guide her breathless gallop. Without realising it and under the cover of night she had crossed the pass and she had scraped the black sky as she peaked it and was now into the next valley. As her legs ran away with her she stumbled and wretched her breath catching in her throat again. Salty and sour. But she did not fall. Something propelled her onwards and then the moon came out from behind a bank of clouds to light her path and the pass was a frozen silver ribbon. A glinting guide – on her side – all the way.

A rapid descent.

But then the cloud returned to deny the moon again and the girl headed towards a darker patch in the landscape – some much-needed cover – still running and stumbling as something once warm and alive but now cold and wet and dead trickled down one leg. A slug-trail along her hairless thigh.

Plants thrashed at her legs and they must have been nettles because soon her calves were burning with a peppery sting; hot and dry with hard white sores rising on the white mottled skin just above the sock line.

The girl paused to stop and scratch and adjust the baby but still she felt a presence behind her. Something up there. Back there. In there. The night.

The smell of that dark bunkhouse shape was strong on her. That man. The sweat and the dirt of him. Whoever he was. His sour skin. His foul stale mouth. The density of him.

She wanted to be sick. She wanted water. She wanted this over.

There were noises out there. Creatures. Nocturnal beasts shifting and watching. Pairs of eyes trained on her from holes and branches and bluffs and crags. She could feel them red and unblinking; the eyes of nature observing. And they no longer felt like allies these creatures. No. Everything was against her now. Even the beasts.

Even the beasts.

The girl ran for the dark patch and stumbled for cover. She pushed her way through thicket and hawthorns and then there was something springing at her jabbing at her stabbing at her a snap of pain a searing through her left eye as a thorn pierced her eyeball. She felt it go in. A rapid insertion. An alien invasion. She thought of hard boiled eggs and burst balloons and wet soap and raw meat.

She flayed and thrashed her arms and her body instinctively drew her back and she felt whatever it was withdraw from her. Pull out from her eyeball. It made a sickening sound in her head. A wet squeak. She thought of rusted nails riven from rotten boards. Exiting rivets and rods. Spikes and skewers. Levering crowbars. She thought of unoiled hinges.

He was unwashed and unshaven yet was wearing an expensive looking tweed coat and when it flapped open he saw that the man was also wearing a dirty white collar. A clerical collar.

He had with him a large panting dog straining at its lead.

Are you open?

His swollen lip impeded his diction.

I'm always open said the Warden.

Are you in charge?

Yes.

I'm here on business said the Priest. Church business.

I thought so. When I saw the dog collar –

I'm looking for a girl. A teenager. She's stolen a baby over in Westmorland. I expect you've heard about it by now.

The Warden hesitated.

Might have heard something from one of the guests. If I can ask: how exactly is this church business Father?

The girl was in my care. She was from the orphanage. Has she been here?

Is this baby hers then?

No. The child belongs to someone else. And the girl took it.

The Warden said nothing.

Harbouring a criminal is an act of criminality said the Priest.

The Warden whistled through his teeth. A shrill sound designed to suggest incredulousness.

That so.

Yes.

The things some people do. Well it looks to me like you could set and rest a while. I never turn a soul away Father – a bit like your place I imagine – and the tea's made so why don't you come in and rest and we'll see what all this is about.

The Priest gave a slight nod and went to enter.

But the dog will have to stay outside I'm afraid. Rules of the house.

It's a working dog said the Priest.

And a fine one I'm sure. But it's council orders – and they pay my wages. Something to do with hygiene. Even in winter they have to stay outside. We've got a nice shed for them. We've had sheep and pigs in there and more besides. One fella stopped by on his way up to Hawes with five dozen ferrets. They went in there an all. Imagine how that looked.

This dog has been deployed to track the scent of the girl said the Priest. I've been tracking her and the child for days and he's led me right to your door.

Well said the Warden. There you go.

So are you going to save my time by answering this one simple question said this determined stranger of the cloth. Have you seen the girl?

In the kitchen the kettle began to whistle.

The Warden casually rubbed the end of his nose.

THE ROCKS WERE arranged in a pile. A man-made monument of sorts. With her one eye and what little light the moon offered the girl saw that it was a miniature cromlech. A burial chamber maybe.

Womb worn neck bruised and half-blind the girl climbed in there and tried to sleep but her perforated eyeball was pulsing and she kept pulling and picking at the gluey strings that were entangling her lashes. Her head howled and her abdomen burned. Fluids ran then dried then others ran again.

The bairn had not made a sound for many hours.

And then the ravenous hunger of the hunted was replaced by nausea and abject despair. The girl could have been presented with a banquet there in her cold stone coffin but she would no longer have been able to eat because the pain in her eye was turning her stomach. Nor would she have fed it to the baby as it was now nothing more than a heap in the corner with a slowing heartbeat. Her thoughts were becoming muddled. Trauma had divested her of logic; the baby was now an impediment. An inanimate thing by her side. It was a footnote to a wider predicament. Just something she had to carry. Purpose forgotten.

A film had formed over her upper and lower eyelids – a grey membrane to shield the perforated ball from infection and the pain was only worsening.

The girl took the dolly rag from her pocket and wedged it into her mouth. She chewed on it hard until her teeth ached and her gums bled and blood dotted the cloth and for a few moments it distracted her from the pain boring through her eye socket and into the back of her skull.

Everyone will exist eternally either in heaven or hell.

When she saw that streaks of pink were stroking sky in the far distance she crawled out from the chamber to shoulder the baby and walked over the next hump of valley flank.

And there it was: the tip of a town creeping round the foot of a mountain one valley over. Through the haze she saw the suggestion of a sleeping stone citadel containing within it houses shops cafes; a place of life and light and electricity. Beyond it the shimmer of a lake two three or more miles away. A civilised corner of this wild cursed land.

With one hand clamped over her eye and the baby on her back the girl let her body take her towards it – towards this new place.

THE SMELL OF paraffin. Sweat streaks running down through the soot on his hands and face and neck.

Behind him the bunk house and everything in it burned like a beacon as the Priest and the dog descended the pass propelled by their own momentum and the heat on their backs.

Let no obstacle stand in the way of duty he said to the dog.

IT IS THE animal that she sees first. A big dog zig-zagging its way down the valley with its nose to the ground. Then thirty paces behind it a triangular figure picking its way over the rocks below her. Too far away to identify.

But she knows. She knows it is him.

She knew he would come.

He was always going to come.

To exert his ownership over her. To claim her. To retain her silence.

The child too. Any congregation child he saw as his.

Wasn't that how he came to own her life all those years ago – when her parents couldn't manage and didn't care and he saw an opportunity to own another person in all ways just like all the others before her and all the others yet to come?

Seeing him the girl felt a strange sense of relief. She knew that he could not creep up on her from behind any more and in fact that was exactly what she could do to him. And that felt powerful. The hunted becomes the hunter. She had the upper hand.

She could turn back and go the way she came. Just flee. Go now. Run forever and maybe never be found.

But not this time. Not with the baby. The baby was *hers* now. She would set it free far away from that town half mad under his rule. Back there it wouldn't stand a chance – not with the feckless Hinckley as a father and his dying wife as a mother. Soon she would be dead and buried and Hinckley wouldn't cope and then the Father and the Sisters would intervene and before anyone knew it he would have his teeth in the child. *Him*. The Priest. Sucking the life out of the young to leave them spent and scared or silent. And on it would go.

But not this time. No. This way there was still hope.

This feeling was new and it was too strong for the girl. A feeling of possibility. Potential. A revelation.

It was too great to ignore. *For it is written: vengeance is mine – I will repay says the Lord.*

And that was when she realised how they all could be free forever.

SO SHE TRACKED him. She stalked him.

Her eye pulsed and wept and her stomach growled and the baby lay inert beneath the overhang of a crag where she had left it but she felt energised for the first time in days.

She watched as the Priest followed the mountain stream downhill. He was three hundred feet or so below her and the stream was flowing strong from the residual seeping of the bogs and marshes up top and the previous day's downpours.

The sound of the water reached her up on the hillside. It would help her. Mask her movements. She moved quickly hunched treading lightly.

And then he stopped where the water widened into a pool. Small but dark and deep. The girl stopped too and ducked behind a rock. She watched as he called the dog and it returned to him. He secured it and then he untied his cape and raised his robe over his head. He looked around and then unbuttoned his shirt and vest and belt and then slowly removed his trousers. Then his underwear.

That was when she started running. Over rocks and down shingle slopes. Through a snatch of bracken then over more slate and shingle. The flat stones moved and shifted underfoot but the Priest did not hear her. The Priest did not turn and the Priest did not look behind him.

She ran towards that white form and saw his skin almost unnaturally pale and hanging off him; his buttocks negligible – nothing more than two frowns at the top of his thin legs.

The girl moved with purpose. She gave herself to the mountain and trusted it for once to let it take her. Guide her. Protect her. Her vision was impaired and her balance was bad but she knew she would not fall.

No. Not this time.

For once everything was on her side. The mountain the stream the rising sun – all had conspired to help her.

She ran closer and the noise of the stream increased: the sound of crisp lines of water breaking on smooth rock. The same sound that had filled the valley for ten thousand years. The sound that had sculpted the land.

She ran with her arms wheeling and her hair bouncing. Only her thighs and calves acted as brakes.

The Priest stepped carefully into the water and then scooped it on his legs and scooped it on his torso and scooped it on his hair and face. She was close enough to see moles on his back now and his thin red hair and the mottling and dimpling of his disgusting flesh. He wobbled forward comically and stooped to steady himself on rocks and the girl thought how vulnerable he looked. How insignificant the Priest suddenly seemed.

How she thought could just one man – one human form – be responsible for so much.

The noise when it came rose from somewhere deep inside her. It was part scream part gurgle and it coursed up through her chest and ripped at her throat. It was primeval it was elemental. Animalistic. She felt it in her entire body. In every cell.

It was louder than the moving water. A banshee's howl than ran down the valley. This time the Priest heard her.

He turned. Wide-eyed and shin-deep. The dog barked. Once twice. Again.

She saw: his concave chest and the curve of his ribs. His penis small and blue and retracted from the ice cold water. His tight scrotum shrivelled like a single walnut. Those thin lips that had worked at her and those elongated nostrils that had sniffed at her. She saw: strands of red hair stuck to a brow that was still dirty from soot and smoke. She saw: the ghost the monster the beast the devil.

A rock. A sharp triangular rock filled her hand.

He scrambled out of the water towards the wailing girl but he could not get his footing and he stumbled.

She went to strike him.

She went to strike him but she let go of her rock at the last moment.

She threw it. She hurled it. The rock.

It hit him above the eye. The sound of stone on bone.

Sickening.

He didn't fall – he buckled. The Priest's legs gave way first and he went to steady himself on the ground then he crumpled sideways like a felled tree. The girl stood over him.

He hadn't made a sound.

She looked at the Priest supine and naked. She took it all in: his hairless shiny shins and the flickering of his lidded eyes; his odd shaped chest neither rising nor falling his limp wrists bent inwards and his fingers curled. Again she looked at his nubby penis so small it seemed incapable of the damage that it had done.

There was no cut. There was neither gash nor wound on his forehead. There was no blood. Only the rapid flowering of his bruising and swelling brow.

But he was dying. She was certain of it. A blow like that could kill anyone. He that had ruled her life and corrupted her life and poisoned her life was in the final throes. And his life – it would soon be over. Because his breath was in his mouth now. He was chewing on it he was gagging on it he was tasting it. His heart was slowing; his system shutting down like night candles being snuffed across the town. And she had done it. She had done this.

The Priest's feet were still in the stream. The water rushed by.

The dog looked on blankly.

13.

SHE ENTERED THE unfamiliar town via a back track that took her down some winding stone steps each slick with damp dawn algae. She clasped a cold metal hand-rail. The flat terrain and clean lines and corners of the buildings felt strange and unnerving after the undulations of the fells. Front gardens were kept trimmed and road signs seemed to be planted or bolted everywhere she looked. Words and arrows and symbols of a sanitised existence. Here the wildness of the fells had been tamed and contained by concrete and cobbles and tarmac and the lives of its inhabitants preserved and framed beneath glass and curtains made of net.

The town was a picturesque jumble of forms – pretty white stone cottages and grey slate municipal buildings amongst spires and parks. It flanked a narrow river with a hump-backed bridge crossing it. In the distance beyond it: more hills more mountains more sky.

It was still early and the girl carried with her the bairn and a leather bag slung over one shoulder. In it there was a knife snare wires fishing hooks string. A thin blanket.

But no food. The remnants of cooked meat and dried fruit and flapjacks were gone. She had eaten them. They had given her the strength to get off the fell.

The bairn had not taken any of it. Its mouth was incapable and its skin was of a strange colouration.

She had not disposed of him. The Priest. She had thought about burying him but that would have required a spade and energy and time and she had none. So she threw his clothes over him and untied the dog and walked away.

The food had made her even hungrier. All she could think about was more food. More meat more fruit more flapjacks – and help for the child.

Sleep and warmth and some milk was all it needed. It was just tired. Yes. There would be help for them here in the town. Yes. The streets were alien and felt strange underfoot. They wouldn't know her here though; they'd think the bairn was hers. She'd get her eye looked at and find a bed for the night. Maybe a bath for the pair of them and she would get their clothes and blankets washed and then in a day or two at the most they would be on their way.

They were just tired. So very very tired.

She gravitated towards the heart of the town – towards that space in the centre and as the girl walked heads turned from those who were up and about early.

They saw a wild-eyed bog girl in her rags. Shuffling stooped and limping – one eye like a small bruised turnip with a scrap of cloth in one hand and a package with a grubby head lolling at her shoulder. Pink scratched welted flesh.

Raw torn cuticle strips. Discoloured teeth and crooked limbs.

Sunken eye shadows grey.

Tattered boots. Chewed lips.

Bone angles.

THE GIRL WITH the red hair who had been sent on the morning's errands saw her hunched on the steps. She recognised something in her. A sympatric familiarity. She saw a need.

Desperation decorated this girl on the steps; it hung from her bones the way she slumped with her head down and her parcel cradled. Dirty and done in. The splattered landscape drying up her legs.

The girl with the red hair approached her with a bag of bread in hand.

Hello.

She looked up and saw the bread. She smelled it – warm and fresh and yeasty. She barely saw the girl with the red hair. All she saw was the bread.

Do you –

She reached for a barm cake and before it was out of the bag it was in the girl's hand. Then it was in her mouth – balled up in in there – stuffed and wedged and moistened and chewed.

Her eye was swollen shut and weeping a purulence that had run and crusted on her cheek. This sorry girl gagged on the bulk of the bread and flour dusted her dry lips but then she put her stout grubby fingers into her mouth and pulled out a wet remnant from her gums and dropped it into the parcel.

Only then did the girl with the red hair see that the parcel was a baby and the baby was not well. Not well at all. The moist chewed bread fell on its face and sat there like a bird dropping. The baby did not respond. The girl scooped up the morsel and then ate it herself. Swallowed again.

Then she exhaled and looked at the girl standing before her who spoke.

Are you alright?

The girl rearranged her parcel. Primped the blanket with a sense of purpose that the red-haired girl found unnerving.

Your child she said again. Perhaps he is hungry. Is it a he?

The girl did not respond. Instead she eyed the bread again.

You should come with me. We can help.

You could have a bath she said.

Get warm she said. Get fed.

You and the baby she said.

Rest a while.

It's safe.

Come.

THE COLD WATER kept him alive. It numbed his feet and forced his blood to slowly circulate and kept his slowing brain alive when all it wanted to do was shut down. Close everything. Kill the signals. But the stream water saved him. The mountain saved him. The swirl of the beck had a rhythm and the Priest's heart locked onto it and it kept beating. It followed the continuance of water over rock and it kept him alive and then when it was ready it shocked him into consciousness.

He awoke with a prayer on his lips. The words sat there before his tongue pushed them out into the world:

One mediator between God and men he rasped. Christ Jesus.

The Priest turned his head to one side. Saw rocks and dirt. His shoes. His clothes were upon him but he was not in them. They were blanketed haphazardly.

He could not feel his feet. The sound of running water. He could not feel them. He could not feel his legs. Panic. He was paralysed. This was it. God had done to him what he had done to the dying Poacher.

An eye for an eye.

He flinched and spasmed and brought his knees up to his chest. He looked down and saw his feet still attached to his legs. He tried to move his toes. He used his brain. He willed them. They moved. Small and white and distant like maggots. He stretched his legs back out and licked his lips. He was thirsty. His head pounded. He propped himself up onto one elbow and looked around.

She did this.

The girl.

Her.

Gone.

The dog untied.

Also gone.

He touched the tips of his fingers to his brow and felt around the curve of his skull. The flesh there had formed a swollen layer that was tender. He pressed gently and it felt unnatural.

Nausea moiled in his stomach. But there was no cut and there was no blood.

It was a miracle.

He saw her coming at him again – screaming – the rock raised like a native with a spear.

He retched a dry heave.

Like a banshee.

In full voice she was. Like a banshee. Only in front of him would she show she had a voice though. That she was capable of making sounds and that sometimes those sounds became words and sometimes those words became sentences. Became speech.

He knew this. Of course he did. He was the only one. He had always known. That was what all of this was about. She held his secrets inside her. She carried them like butterflies in a jar and one day she would let them out with her mouth. She would start talking and she would never stop and some would claim it a miracle and others would just sit and listen. And then they would come and find him.

There were things she had been privy to; things he had confided in the darkest early hours. Things she had had done to her that should never be turned into noise into words and sentences and speech. Church business. Bedroom business. His business.

She held these things over him. He knew it and she knew it. She had that power. That was why she had to be stopped contained confined. Watched over. The child was his excuse; his justification. He didn't care about some stupid mewling baby – the world was full of them. He cared about his status. He cared about his freedom. He cared about keeping her mute and passive and under his control. He cared about keeping all of them mute and passive and under his control though she was the first to flee.

He retched again and this time a string of saliva hung from his mouth. A groan followed it. He moved up onto a second elbow and wiped his mouth. He remembered he still had another vial in his trouser pocket.

He checked it. It was there.

LOGS CRACKLED IN the fire. Embers danced in the updraught and a soft black fur-like layer of soot coated the inside of the chimney breast where it wavered in the rising air.

The room was snug; the room was warm. There were old varnished shelves with books on them and framed pictures of animals. Pencil drawings of cows in a field; sheep pigs a fox. Implements were hung on the wall too. A brass bed-warmer and horseshoes and an old hunting horn.

There had been none of these decorations at St Mary's. At St Mary's they would have been considered vain and sinful. Gaudy.

Treasures of wickedness profit nothing.

The girl with the red hair led her to the fire then pulled a chair in close for her. She was limping badly and her eye was still weeping.

It had taken the last of her energy to follow the girl with the bread to the workhouse. Still the child had not stirred.

Cradling her parcel she sat in front of the fire and within a minute was asleep. Her cheeks flushed from the heat of the flames. The silent parcel still clutched to the chest.

The girl watched for a moment then she left the room and quietly closed the door behind her.

Even though it had passed through the villages and hamlets she did not know about the story that had crossed Westmorland and Cumberland like an August heather blaze – that of the young church girl who had stolen a child and gone on the run.

Some said the baby was needed for a sacrificial ritual that was to take place in the stone circle at Castlerigg; some said the girl had gone devil-possessed and had killed it herself. Some said the bairn wasn't even the Hinckleys'. Others speculated that it was most likely the baby was being spirited away to the coast where it would be sold abroad – to the dark continent – where white children like this one were more valuable than gold or diamonds and that the dummy girl was being paid to transport it to a boat docked off Whitehaven.

There was talk of the priest too. They said he would see the safe return of the child; others said there was never smoke without fire – and smoke followed that one like a coffin nail.

The girl with the red hair had not heard any of this but the woman who ran the workhouse had. Miss Mullen.

She was in her office when there was a knock on her door. It was one of her girls back from her errands and holding a bag of bread now depleted.

There's another one Miss Mullen. Another lass.

She looked up from her papers.

What do you mean Dulcie?

I found another girl. Up on the ginnel steps while fetching the messages. She's got a bairn with her and a right gammy eye. She's barely fit to stand. Half dead the both of them.

Where is she?

I brought her back and put her in the reading room. In front of the fire to get a warm.

Good – that was the Christian thing to do. You say she's got a child with her?

More like a baby.

Show me.

WASP-STUNG BITTER-MOUTHED AND unsteady he trained his feet towards the town and got to walking.

As he walked he talked. Muttered to himself.

No said the Priest. No. She cannot be allowed to get away with this. Any of this. Retribution is due.

He stopped to retch. He doubled over. His head pounded and the pain ran down one side of his head and into his neck.

No no no no no.

He straightened up

No.

Not her not the girl not the one they think is a dummy. After all this – she cannot be the one that brings you down. No. Not her. Not that useless smelly Godless lump. No. Of all the girls that have passed through St Mary's – not her.

He was on a discernible path now. A path made of uneven flagstones with clusters of grass growing from the cracks. The path would take him to the town. The town would take him to the girl. The girl would have a tongue. He would take that tongue and he would rip it out and roast it on a spit and make sure she could never speak of Church business – his business – to anyone.

And the baby he said out loud. Let the baby burn in hell too.

THE LORD REIGNS let the earth rejoice; let the islands be glad.

She was there. She was on that island. The two of them. The island looked like one of the mountains in which she had spent her entire life but this time it was different. This time the mountain was surrounded by water. Water as far as the eye could see. On the mountain there were caves and animals and tarns and woods and waterfalls and one house made from branches and another made up a tree. A fire always burned and the bairn was strong and silent and healthy and as another day ended together they sat looking out to sea as the red sun settled behind it.

Death shall be no more neither shall there be mourning nor crying, nor pain anymore for the former things have passed away.

She awoke in a panic and her face burning with the beginnings of a fever. She was in a chair in an unfamiliar room surrounded by animal prints and rural ephemera.

The bairn was gone.

She stood but her legs gave as the blood drained from her head. She stooped and leaned against the back of the chair to catch her breath.

The child.

The child.

My child.

She pushed herself away from the chair and pulled herself along bookshelves. Weak leg joints aching dizzy sickness.

Fever and confusion.

The baby.

They could not take the bairn.

The door handle felt ice cold in her hot hand.

It led to a corridor with wooden floors and many many doors. She tried one. It was a storage cupboard with mop bucket dusters polish. The next door was locked. The third opened into a large dormitory with bunk beds and the strong smell of disinfectant. There was no-one in it. She lurched down the corridor.

The baby. The bairn.

The next door she tried contained toilets and sinks. Two girls were in there – one brushing her teeth and the other combing her hair. Another mop and bucket leaned against the white tiled wall beside them. They turned to look at her and their faces registered surprise then one of them said something that the girl didn't catch and they laughed.

At the next door more voices. Females. Two of them. She wiped pus from her cheek then pressed an ear to the door. Voices.

Is it her?

I don't know.

She fits the description.

Lots of girls would.

But in that state.

I know.

Coming down from the fells like that.

And mute with it.

And mute with it.

Young Dulcie says she never uttered a word.

You know she opened her eyes when I went in and even the look of her's odd. It was like she was seeing right through me. Turned me cold.

Well there's something up with one of her eyes.

I know but it wasn't that. It was something else. It was like she was in another world. Or sent from another place. Maybe it's true what they say about the devil being in her.

Lord only knows what's been going on but let's not fall foul of hearsay.

And that bairn.

Yes. That poor child. Look at it.

It must be her. The one they're after. Has to be.

This child is in a poor state.

It barely has a pulse.

Abducted or not it needs attention. Now. For its own safety.

Naturally.

That's a priority.

They're our responsibility. But we've not got the facilities for this.

No.

The poor thing.

I know.

What its been through.

Miles they must have travelled.

And not by transport by the look of her shoes.

On hands and knees more like.

Sleeping rough.

Taking someone's child from under their nose.

A baby needs regular feeds. Stability. Hygiene.

Disgraceful.

She'll be a long time locked up when the judge gets to her.

At this the girl flinched but still she kept listening.

And what of that child said the voice muted by the wood of the door which she pressed herself to.

It'll be back with its mother and father where it belongs of course.

We don't know it's her though. Not for certain.

It has to be.

It could be.

It has to be.

At this the girl pushed the door open and the women stopped talking.

The baby was there with them in a cot beside the desk. Both of the women were standing by the cot and looking into it.

The girl's eye was weeping a stream of sticky yellow fluid and her clothes were hanging off her. They saw a pathetic figure.

She took a step forward and held out her arms at waist height.

What does she want said the first woman. Miss Pegg.

She wants the bairn said the other. Mullen. Miss Mullen.

They spoke as if she was not there.

It's resting the first one said. And you'll be minded to do the same. Until the doctor gets here.

Yes we've called for the doctor said Miss Mullen. She exaggerated the words in her mouth as if speaking to someone deaf. We've. Called. For. The. Doctor. For the both of you. That eye needs looking at.

The girl held out her arms to receive what was hers.

Is it yours?

The baby said the other woman. Is it yours?

The girl nodded and then moved forward to pick the bairn up from its cot.

Miss Pegg put a hand on her shoulder.

I'm not sure you should be doing that. The child needs rest. You're in God's house now; you'll be looked after.

The girl ignored her and lifted the child from beneath its blanket and held it to her chest. Then she took out a breast and held a nipple to the baby's mouth. It rested there for a moment. The bairn's lips quivered ever so slightly and then it took the girl's teat.

Look Miss Mullen.

I can see.

As the women watched the baby suckled. Milk ran from the side of its mouth.

She's milking said Miss Pegg. Look: the baby is taking it like it's the most natural thing. Maybe it is hers after all.

Maybe said Miss Mullen.

The bairn's taking it. It's like a miracle.

Yes.

But she's so dirty.

Filthy.

They spoke to the girl now.

If you're going to do that you need to be bathed and clean said Miss Mullen. There's ways of doing things and this isn't one of them.

The woman continued to speak as if the girl was deaf.

In the meantime there's fresh milk in the kitchen. Let us get you back in front of the fire. Miss Pegg – have some milk warmed up and bottled. Proper milk. And get some more blankets. Water soap and rags too.

That eye needs looking at said Miss Pegg.

It does. But first the child.

Miss Pegg left.

The doctor will be here within the hour.

Miss Mullen put an arm around the girl and steered the girl and the suckling child towards the door.

Come with me. I'll take you back to the reading room. We'll get you fed and cleaned and the doctor can take a look at you. You're lucky you found us.

Or we found you. Or God found us all. For He sees everything.

THIS TOWN. HE had been here before. The last time was two years ago. It was a different parish but the same diocese. Father Raymond ran things.

He knew Father Raymond to be a maverick too. Like him he only answered to God. They didn't let the church dictate all their rules; only God had their attention. And they shared the same taste for the unconventional. Father Raymond understood. Father Raymond was devout. Father Raymond kept a tight ship. Hadn't he at Raymond's invitation visited St Joseph's Shelter for Fallen Women? Yes. Many a winter's night he had spent there snowed in and holed up. Instructing the women.

Yes. Raymond tolerated his ways. Because he knew it was all for a greater good.

The Priest limped onwards. His clothes bedraggled and buttoned up incorrectly.

Yes. He would pay Father Raymond a visit when this issue was resolved. That was what he would do. He would pay them all a visit. Raymond and his Sisters. Maybe rest up there for a while. Let the dust settle and rumour wither on the vine. He would re-charge re-connect with an extended flock. Father Raymond could be trusted. He was one of the old guard who respected the old ways. He was one of the very few.

They'd thank him for all this. For finding the girl. The child – well the people wanted its safe return but it would be the finding and punishing of the girl that they would favour. Yes. This he knew. That was all that really mattered to them.

Because his congregation valued him. They genuflected to his deep understanding of the scriptures; were as servile as a community should be. Not everyone was like that idiot Poacher or that fetid troglodyte. Theological knowledge still meant something to a lot of people around these parts. And weaknesses were accepted. Sometimes they were even indulged. Supplied. Because he was after all God's representative and such a role carried heavy burdens. Few humans could shoulder it without buckling now and again. They understood that no man is perfect. Because if he was then he would not be a man.

BUT SHE DIDN'T need to see a doctor. He wouldn't know what she knew – that something had irrevocably changed and not just her dying useless eye.

Something was inside of her now. Something else. A burning and a growing. A newness. An other.

Another.

It had only been a matter of hours but life was already happening. Cells were gathering. Life was germinating like a seedling.

She had a fever and she was starving. She was cut and blistered and dehydrated and suffering from severe malnutrition and exposure and the onset of influenza but she felt this new life within her. Something of her own. It over-rode everything else.

Already it was growing. Something inside of her to love and pet and protect; something that was part her. Part *of* her. It had been forced upon her in the night but the beginnings didn't matter – only what came later. She always knew she had the capacity. Hadn't the beastings shown her so – that her body was ready? That when food or drink or milk or shelter was needed nature always provided. And when something to nurture and love and escape through was needed then that was provided too.

In time the who and when and how she was seeded would be forgotten because now she would have something of her own. A family. Not a cuckoo child but one of her very own.

God had tested her by showing her Hinckley and the child and the open door and the fells beyond it and when she had passed the test he had sent a fresh seed and now no-one would ever be able to take that away.

Children are a gift from the Lord; they are a reward from Him.

Yes. Everything would be different from now. Yes. Everything would be better. She would be free. Unmolested. Inviolate.

Yes.

And He – he was gone. His heart no longer beat and He would never again put his hands on her. None of them would. Farmers fathers priests and bunkhouse strangers. She instinctively knew that she was with child and everyone knows no-one touches a woman with child. For it is written.

Her lips silently mouthed the words: and the beast was taken – and with him the false prophet that wrought miracles before him – with which he deceived them that had received the mark of the beast and them that worshipped his image. These both were cast alive into a lake of fire burning with brimstone.

There was a future.

She saw it.

THE PRIEST WALKED through town. Mud streaked the hem of his coat. He looked fell-weary and feverish. Soiled yet barbarous.

It was mid morning – a week day – and the market was busy. He stopped at a fruit and vegetable stall and bought two apples then bolted them. He walked on. There was a stall selling dried goods. Fruit chutneys preserves. He bought nuts from the woman running it. She handed him his change and when his coat fell open and she saw his collar she spoke.

Sorry father. I didn't realise she said.

Realise what?

That you're of the cloth.

What difference does it make?

I always like to gift a small something to God's people. His harvest is how I make my living.

She bent down and pulled out a small wrapped parcel.

The Priest stared at the stall-holder. Said nothing.

She passed the parcel to him and he took it.

Is it business that brings you here to our town Father?

Yes.

She sniffed.

Of course your business is your business.

I'm here about one of my parishioners.

Not the missing girl is it Father?

Which missing girl?

The one everyone's talking about. The one I reckon to have walked by the stall not but an hour or less since.

Is she alive?

His voice rasped as he said this.

Reckon she must be said the woman.

Where is she now?

Know her well do you?

I thought you said my business was my business.

I expect you'll know where to find her then Father.

Joseph's?

Not for me to say Father.

Joseph's then.

Expect you know where to find that too.

Yes.

He turned to leave.

Father? said the stall-holder.

Yes?

Seems a bit strange you'd come all this way and not even ask about the wee one she was carrying across her back.

He turned and left.

MISS MULLEN SAT the girl down and put more logs on the fire and pulled the blanket over her and told her that she would be back before the doctor arrived with milk and maybe some cold apple sauce left over from Sunday for the child.

She met Miss Pegg at the bottom of the stairs. She took the bottle of milk and more blankets from her and instructed her to mind the girls who had long finished their breakfast and were already getting restless over rumours of a new arrival.

There was a knock at the door which they both answered. It was the doctor. Killip. The best in town. The only in town.

Then right behind him two policemen. One they recognised as one of the Daldry brothers. The other was young and not from town. A new recruit probably.

Doctor said Miss Mullen. Officers.

Is it her? said Daldry.

The lass that's stole the bairn? asked the new recruit.

The policemen tried to squeeze past the doctor but the doorstep was too crowded and there was a brief awkward moment as bodies collided then Daldry pulled rank and stepped through with purpose.

We think so said Miss Pegg.

We don't know that for sure said Miss Mullen. Could just be that she's a stray. She acts like the bairn's hers.

The young policeman snorted.

We'll find out right enough said Daldry. Where's the girl?

She's indoors.

The doctor said nothing.

And the bairn?

With her.

What about the parents of the bairn?

They've been notified.

Take me to her said Daldry.

HE LEANED AGAINST THE railings and opened his coat. He ducked his head and took a long sniff from the vial. It was nearly empty. He was down to the final white grains. The town felt crooked. Askance. Like it had no centre or its point of gravity was constantly shifting. Variable. Like it was a new version of itself. He walked along the road to St Joseph's. There were people at the door. Police. He walked past them then turned left down the side street and entered through the back door. There was a renewed urgency in his stride. The powder gave him strength and clarity but he knew it would wear off soon.

He walked through the kitchens and down the corridor turning door handles and putting his head round doors to look in rooms moving swiftly and economically and precisely; his mouth dry his pulse racing his temples throbbing. He saw girls cleaning. He saw girls scrubbing. Girls half undressed. Girls surprised girls distressed. He quickened his step. He tried more doors. He found the right door. He entered the door. He closed the door behind him.

A SCREAM. THERE was a scream to ice the blood and turn hairs white. A scream to stop clocks. A sound that seemed to come from nothing human.

The howl was long and sharp and barbed and made of delicate crystal. It cut through the building and down corridors. Everyone heard it – the girls the staff the doctor the police – and even after it ended it hung in the air a moment before it fell to the floor shattering in shards of pain. Fragments of despair.

Feet rattled across floorboards in competition to reach the source of the sound first. And then bodies were crowding the room. The two women and the three men of authority. The room seemed to shrink in size. It became a hot tight space. The air singed with the scent of something acrid.

The girl was curled on the floor by the hearth. Hunched and foetal and quivering lightly.

And there was a man there too. A priest. A stranger. He was standing over her. A man they did not know. An ugly man. A wild panting man. A man with a collar and a bruised face tight like a death mask.

His hands were held in loose fists by his side and his slitted nostrils were flaring like those of an animal that has detected a scent on the spring breeze. There were scratches down the side of his face. Great fresh wet gashes. The skin around them was red. He was breathing heavily. Beside him on the chair was a blanketed heap.

Where's the child said Daldry. And who are you?

The Priest stared back. He stayed silent.

What have you done? said Miss Mullen.

She moved towards the girl and she put a hand on her shoulder and then she carefully rolled the girl over to her.

They saw that her top was undone and her breasts were bared. They were white sagging things that spread flat across her chest as she turned onto her back and one of them had tiny shining traces of milk around the darkened teat. The droplets looked like jewels. Like diamonds.

Only then did they see her hands. They were two smoking shapeless stumps. They were stripped and blistered and trembling. The fingers were gone now and what remained had melded into two inverted waxy claws. The girl's hands were spent candles dripping skin.

Miss Mullen gasped – they all did – and the girl stared upwards. Her face advertised surprise that there were several people there in the room with her. The flames were reflected in the shine of feverish sweat on her upper lip and strands of hair were stuck to her brow and the back of her neck. She turned and blinked and took them in. One eye was sealed and swollen like an exotic fruit but the other was wide and wild and dark and alert. Her ruined hands were held up before her.

Miss Mullen went to touch the girl but she flinched and seemed to shake harder and the moment was one of such surprise and revulsion that no-one else moved then the fire cracked and popped loudly and broke the frozen seconds.

You said Daldry. His voice trembled as he pointed towards the Priest and said: your name.

The wages of sin is death said the Priest. But the free gift of God is eternal life in Christ Jesus our Lord.

As Miss Mullen reached for the girl again Miss Pegg stepped forward to the chair. She pulled back the blanket. Beneath it were rags and a dirty knotted piece of cloth. The dolly rag.

The child she said. Where is it?

Behold said the Priest. Children are a gift of God – the fruit of the womb – a reward. And so we give back unto you. Praise the Lord.

The bairn said Daldry.

The girl was shaking. The girl was rattling. Her tongue ran across dry cracked lips and still her hands were held in front of her and a gruff sound caught in her throat. It squirmed there. It gurgled there.

The bairn said Miss Mullen.

Where've you hidden it said Miss Pegg.

The girl raised her head and licked her lips again.

What bairn she said.

She spoke said Miss Mullen. She –

The Priest turned to the fire. They all did. It was roaring and crackling with a renewed hunger. They saw what the girl saw. A blazing bundle. A new form within the raging flames.

Amen said the Priest.